LIVE AND
LOVE AGAIN

Visit us at www.boldstrokesbooks.com

LIVE AND LOVE AGAIN

by

Jan Gayle

2016

LIVE AND LOVE AGAIN

ISBN 13: 978-1-62639-517-6

THIS TRADE PAPERBACK ORIGINAL IS PUBLISHED BY
BOLD STROKES BOOKS, INC.
P.O. BOX 249
VALLEY FALLS, NY 12185

FIRST EDITION: JANUARY 2016

CREDITS
EDITOR: CINDY CRESAP
PRODUCTION DESIGN: SUSAN RAMUNDO
COVER DESIGN BY GABRIELLE PENDERGRAST

Acknowledgments

Kate Horsley, author, teacher, mentor, and friend. Thank you for your support and encouragement. Christie DeVaul, my ideal reader. You are an amazing sis-in-law; thank you for being the first to read my stories. Kim Emerson, author and publisher. I would have never believed in my story without your positive words and assistance.

Dedication

To my beautiful wife, Jules, who always stands beside me.

CHAPTER ONE

The long, winding line moved forward, and Sarah stepped closer. She felt the muscles in her shoulders and around her neck tighten. Her hands grew moist with sweat, and her heart rate increased. Only three people separated her from the tall, skinny podium. With her ticket and identification in hand, she was as prepared as she could be. Besides, she told herself, they were only TSA agents—poorly trained and underpaid—amateur airport security.

Sarah hated airports and flying. She wasn't scared of flying; she just hated the process and the anxiety it caused her. The events of 9/11 had put in place mostly ineffective security measures that added a whole new level of stress to traveling. And Sarah's previous active duty military experience made the process even more frustrating, because she knew how truly inadequate the security measures were. She even had a major run-in with some TSA agents in the past. On a return trip from Albuquerque to Phoenix, she had gotten frustrated with them after they ran her bag through the metal detector for the third time and still wouldn't let her open it so she could show them that the offending object was a metal tin of cookies, a gift for her niece. The angrier she got, the more they examined her items until they nearly made her miss her flight—all over some stupid cookies. Comforted by claiming as much control over her experiences as possible, she gave herself an excessive amount of time to get through those lame security procedures.

It was just now five in the morning, and Sarah had already been up for an hour and a half. There was a chill in the air when she left her house in Chandler to drive the thirty minutes to the Phoenix Sky Harbor airport. She had been waiting for the cool mornings for several weeks now. This was the reason she stayed here. That and she didn't believe she could leave—even when the hot, dry summers dragged on into November.

The cool she felt when she left hadn't warranted the lined trench coat that lay over her arm, but she knew she would need it before the day was over. When she dug it out of the back of the closet late last night, she was relieved she had kept it. The weather in the greater Phoenix area rarely got cold enough for a jacket of any kind, let alone a big winter coat. Also, a formal coat was really not practical for her. In the last five years, she could count on one hand the number of times she had worn anything but jeans or maybe the occasional pair of slacks. She even had to spend last weekend in a crowded, stuffy mall to get the suit she wore today. She coaxed her friends Patricia and Christine to go with her to make sure she didn't buy pants that were better suited for a 1980s disco—the last time she had paid much attention to clothes—than an important business meeting. Christine was a lawyer and wore suits every day, and Patricia just had a great sense of style. Although she caused them much consternation in the process, they outfitted her quite well, but the impact to her wallet was far greater than she had expected.

Despite the fact that Patricia said everything fit her perfectly, her suit coat was as constricting as a straitjacket across her shoulders. Her pants felt so tight she feared sitting, and her feet were already sore after only wearing the heels for a couple of hours. Even so, she felt professional and...tall. That was exactly what she was going for—the professional part anyway. She knew from experience that feeling the part was half the battle in pulling it off. *This is a good move. It's exactly what I need. If only I didn't have to go through airports to get there.*

Sitting at the gate, waiting impatiently for the moment when she could get on the plane and relax, Sarah pulled herself upright against the back of the chair working hard to look like a professional. Because what she really felt was that heavy, dragging feeling that comes from not getting enough sleep. She was hoping she would sleep for the three and a half hour flight to Chicago. For once, she had granted herself a rare luxury, a first-class upgrade. She was confident this trip was going to be a success, and she would make a little extra cash. It was odd to think she might have extra money, something that had eluded her lately. She realized she was lucky, because she always had what she needed, but there were some pretty close calls over the last couple of years.

While she waited, two agents approached the counter in front of Sarah's gate and went through a routine of turning on computers, flipping through papers, and moving velvet cables. Sarah got up and moved slowly toward the gate, rolling her small carry-on bag behind her. With her upgrade, she'd be a part of the first to board. Then she could find her seat and get ready to snooze even though she most likely wouldn't be able to get too comfortable in her business suit. And there would be no time to freshen up before her first official meeting with Meyer Furniture Design Incorporated, scheduled for two this afternoon. Several weeks of long hours, both in the workshop and in front of her computer preparing for this meeting, had kicked her butt. Sarah had wanted...needed to stay busy though, so she didn't mind so much. Keeping busy was the only way to avoid thinking about the past, to keep grief at arm's length, to not feel how empty those arms were now.

Sarah's attention was drawn away from the agents when she heard that familiar clicking sound of high heels on a hard tile floor. The two men in front of her turned their heads, and they all stared. The woman moving in their direction wore a midnight blue dress with a matching, perfectly tailored jacket. The dress's hem fell high on her thigh, accentuating her shapely, long legs extended by high, black leather heels. She stood tall, carrying an expensive leather briefcase over one shoulder and pulling her carry-on bag behind her. Sarah backed up slightly to let her pass and caught a scent of her dark, subtle perfume as she breezed past toward the counter.

While Sarah was distracted, the agent called for first-class passengers to board, and she found herself at the end of the premiere passenger line. She didn't mind so much. She was fascinated with this woman and wanted to observe her for just a moment longer. Her beautiful olive complexion was flawless and highlighted the perfect deep red tone on her lips. Her dark chocolate brown hair was pulled up loosely. A few wavy strands escaped and were lying against her elegant, long neck. Sarah knew she was staring, but she didn't stop herself. That type of allure was hard to deny. For a second, Sarah imagined her legs wrapped around this woman. She had worked hard to not fantasize about sex with straight women. It only led to frustration, but the thought passed through her mind like a breeze as she watched her.

"Good morning." Sarah heard the woman greet the agent, who didn't look up when she spoke. "Please give me your full attention for just a few moments."

The agent glanced over at her companion and shrugged, and then cocked her head to look over her glasses. "What is it?" "I purchased a first-class ticket. Just now at the automated check-in machine, this ticket was printed." She held up the ticket and continued. "Perhaps you could take just a minute and print the correct ticket for me." The agent grabbed the ticket and examined it. "I think first-class is full."

"I'll wait here until you can resolve the problem," the woman said with no emotion.

Sarah squirmed a bit when she heard the exchange between the two women. She was slightly concerned about her own seat. She paid the extra money for the first-class ticket just this morning using the machine at the ticket counter. Suspicious of automated systems, she worried she might lose it to this lady. Sarah had never trusted those automated systems. That machine could have given Sarah someone else's seat. It didn't matter how hot this woman was, Sarah was not giving up her comfortable seat—not today.

The agent pushed a few buttons and within seconds produced another ticket. She handed it to the passenger without looking up.

"Thank you so much." The woman paused. When there was no response from the agent behind the counter she continued, "It seems you're having the same kind of morning as I am, but I believe the day is about to get better for both of us." She turned, and with heels clicking, she filed in behind Sarah.

The agent looked up, and Sarah saw her smile for the first time all morning. Sarah was somewhat amazed at how things worked out. It never seemed to be so simple and easy when something like that happened to her. She could tell the woman was clearly accustomed to getting what she wanted.

Sarah settled into her window seat, and much to her surprise and delight the dark, good-looking woman took her place in the seat next to her. As she sat down, Sarah was no longer in a position to stare without being seen, but she couldn't help notice her thin, sexy legs as she settled into the comfortable first-class seat. Sarah enjoyed talking to new people, but the thought of talking to a woman so stunning sent a tight feeling of panic through her chest. She fumbled with the seat belt trying to think of something to say. She was so absorbed in thought that she was startled when the flight attendant, who had been hovering over them, spoke. "What can I get you to drink?" Several coach passengers were standing in the aisle waiting for the flight attendant to move. Sarah hated how they always tried serving the first-class guests drinks while the coach passengers were still boarding.

"Mimosa and a Pellegrino with a lime, no ice," the woman rattled off.

"And for you, ma'am?"

"I'll just have water." The flight attendant nodded and moved quickly back to the galley to fix the drinks. The flow of passengers resumed.

The woman turned to Sarah and sighed. "I hate these early morning flights, but I had no choice today. I have to be in Chicago before two. My name is Jessica, by the way. You have wonderful eyes."

"Thank you. I'm Sarah. Me too. I mean...same exactly. I mean...I have to be in Chicago at two also," Sarah stammered as she looked into mesmerizing eyes so dark they looked like little pools of ink. She caught herself staring and looked down at her lap.

"That's an interesting coincidence. Why do you have to be in Chicago?" Jessica began setting up her laptop.

The flight attendant returned with their drinks. "Ma'am, your water and, ma'am, your mimosa and..." Just as the attendant bent to hand Jessica her mimosa, the Pellegrino slid off the tray and splashed all over the bottom of Jessica's dress, her legs, and her shoes.

"Oh no, ma'am! I'm so sorry. I'll get some towels." The flight attendant squealed with big eyes and arms flailing around. She nearly dropped the tray on Jessica's head as she tried to pick up the glass and lime.

Jessica touched her on the shoulder. "It's okay. Relax."

"No, ma'am, it's not. I'm such a klutz. I'll get taken off of first-class."

"That's ridiculous. It was an accident, and it was only water." Jessica looked up at the attendant while she was still moving aimlessly. "Just bring me a towel and another Pellegrino after you've served the other passengers. It's fine."

"Yes, ma'am." She somehow gained her composure. She returned immediately with the towel and another glass of mineral water.

"Thank you so much." Jessica wiped her leg and dabbed at her dress. "It will be dry in just a few minutes." She handed the towel back to the flight attendant. "It's going to be okay. What is your last name, Jean?" She read her name tag.

"Matthews." She looked confused.

Jessica opened her iPad and jotted a note, and then glanced at Sarah who was silently observing the event. "There was a little unexpected excitement. Now, what was I saying? Ah, you were about to tell me what you were going to be doing in Chicago."

"You handled that so well. She was afraid you were going to yell at her."

"What good would that have done?"

"Exactly." Sarah pondered a minute. "Yeah…ah…I design and build custom furniture, and some of my designs are being considered for production and retail sale. You?" Sarah was torn between her desire to snuggle up in the corner and the desire to get to know this gorgeous woman sitting next to her.

"Really? I mean, that's wonderful. Tell me about what you design and what you build." Jessica flashed a white smile, and Sarah was no longer torn or tired.

"Oh no. Wait, you didn't tell me what you do." Sarah teased her a little.

Again, that smile. "I'm an architect, and as much as I would prefer to be designing, somehow, I've worked myself into a position where I sit in meetings with old, fat men winning contracts, leaving me very little time to do what I love." She shrugged. "Back to your furniture."

Sarah loved to talk about her work, but she rarely found someone who genuinely wanted to hear about it. She often caught herself explaining in great detail the quality of different types of wood and quickly losing the interest of everyone around her, but Jessica seemed truly fascinated. Sarah started with the big picture. "I own and operate a small, custom furniture business. I build pretty much anything from tables and bookcases to cabinets and bedroom sets. That's what pays the bills." She stopped and saw that Jessica was listening intently so she continued. "But what I really love is designing one-of-a-kind wood art."

"I would love to see some of your work. Do you have photos I could look at?" Jessica closed her laptop and slid it back into her briefcase.

Sarah pulled out her own small laptop and opened the presentation she had prepared for today. "I was recently… discovered." She laughed.

Jessica pulled Sarah's laptop over to her own tray table and stared at the screen. "This is wonderful. Absolutely amazing. You do this all yourself?"

"Yeah."

"Who are you showing this to, and is it for sale?" Jessica was examining each piece.

"Don't look too closely. I'm afraid you'll find a flaw." But Sarah knew each piece was perfect. "The owner of Meyer Furniture Design saw me at an art show. I traveled up to Santa Fe this spring for a show just to see how my work compared. I had designed a unique and modern dry bar for a customer last winter, and he let me take it to the show. Bryan Meyer, the owner of the company, saw me at the show and wanted to buy the design to reproduce and sell in his stores."

"I can understand why he would be interested."

"I wasn't sure at first if I wanted to sell it to be mass produced. It was built to be a custom piece, but when he offered me the possibility of a contract for more designs, I really couldn't turn him down. I can make ends meet building custom projects locally, but I couldn't resist the security of his offer. And it would give me time to design more. So that's why I'm going to Chicago—to show him these designs. Hopefully, I sell these pieces and get a contract for more."

"Sarah, you're an amazing artist."

"Thank you. I've never really thought of myself as an artist, but I like the sound of it." Sarah was beginning to feel a little embarrassed at all the attention. "So what about you? Are you from Phoenix or Chicago?"

"I'm from Chicago, born and raised. I can't imagine ever leaving. I work for a great firm. We've designed buildings all over the Midwest and some Eastern cities. I would like for us to have a presence in the West as well. I was in Phoenix working on winning a contract there—actually trying to steal it, but that sounds worse than it really is." She explained her recent trip to Phoenix and showed Sarah a few sketches of the designs for the building she hoped to win for her company.

"Wow, that's a huge building. I had no idea they were constructing something that impressive downtown."

"It will be a great composition for the Phoenix skyline if they choose the right architect." She smiled.

"I'm sure they will." Sarah gave her a knowing grin.

"Do you have your own workshop?"

"I do. I have everything you could possibly want to build anything—power tools, hand tools, the works."

"Do you employ anyone?"

Sarah laughed. "If you count the neighbor kid who helps me deliver heavy furniture sometimes." She thought for a second. "I can't imagine ever being in a position to need to hire someone."

"Sarah, if you marketed to the right people you would have more work than you could possibly do alone."

Sarah was embarrassed again and quickly changed the subject. "How long were you in Phoenix?"

"I flew in Monday, met with the group and presented my proposal on Tuesday, and I'm now on my way back home."

"That's a quick trip. No time to enjoy our warm fall. Did you have time to do anything?"

"No. Unfortunately, I only saw the inside of business offices, but I'm planning a few more trips out here so perhaps I'll take in some sites then. What about you? Are you from Phoenix originally?"

"No, actually, I'm from Illinois—not Chicago though."

"Small world. Where in Illinois?"

"I'm from a farm community south of Springfield."

"Interesting, I'm sad to say I don't know much about the rest of the state," Jessica admitted. "How'd you end up in Phoenix?"

"The Air Force sent me there, and after I retired, I stayed."

"You were in the Air Force? You're full of surprises. And you're retired?"

"I retired about five years ago."

"Thank you so much for your service."

Sarah just smiled and nodded humbly. She never knew what to say to that.

Before Sarah realized it, three hours had passed. They had talked nonstop the entire flight. "It was great talking with you. You helped make the time go by quickly. I truly hate flying, and I hardly knew I was in the air. Thanks," Sarah said as she buckled her seat belt.

Jessica buckled her own belt. "How are you getting downtown for your meeting?"

"I'm just going to grab a taxi." Sarah barely got out the word taxi before Jessica jumped in.

"No, you are not! That will cost a fortune. You're riding with me."

Sarah hesitated a bit. "I couldn't impose on you. The taxi is fine."

"Sarah, I insist. Look, the company car is picking me up anyway. The building you're going to is just down the street from our offices. Seriously, I won't let you take a taxi."

Again, Sarah wiggled uncomfortably in her seat. She couldn't remember telling Jessica what building her meeting was in. "Okay. Thank you. That's very kind." She really wasn't accustomed to people being so generous, but the thought of spending a few more minutes with Jessica made the decision easier. She liked her a lot. It was a little scary to be so attracted to someone, to really want to get to know them. It had been a long time.

❖

Jessica knew she had to think of something or Sarah was going to walk out of her life. Jessica had noticed Sarah when she brushed past her at the airport gate to correct the last problem in her unusually crazy morning.

Jessica maintained a color-coded, automated calendar on her iPad, and her secretary was the only person with access. She always knew how every minute of every day was to be spent, so it was rare for anything to be slightly out of place, let alone go as badly as they had this morning. First, the service failed to call her and she overslept. Then, because she overslept, the car she arranged to take her to the airport was stolen from her by another guest at the Ritz. He apparently felt entitled to it. So when she arrived at the airport and was presented with a coach ticket, she was about ready to explode.

Jessica noticed Sarah again when she was waiting in the first-class line to board the flight. She really got a chance to appreciate her as she watched her walk in front of her down the jet way to the plane. Sarah wore a fitted taupe suit and beige heels. Her slacks hung low on her slim hips, and the short jacket length allowed Jessica to have a perfect view of her shapely, tight butt. Her long auburn hair was pulled into a soft ponytail at the back of her neck and clipped with a simple but elegant barrette. Jessica imagined waking up with that silky red hair across her chest, and she felt a familiar hot rush in her lower body.

She had a chance to really get to know her on the flight when fate sat them next to each other. Now she needed to think of a way to spend more time with her. Maybe she could even ask her on a date. She had thought of the car ride at the last minute. Not only could she help out a new friend, she could also buy herself another thirty minutes to get brave enough to ask her out.

Bravery was not normally a quality Jessica lacked, but even at thirty-eight, she still got nervous when it came to asking a beautiful woman out to dinner. Jessica was sure Sarah was a lesbian, but she had learned her lesson years ago about stereotyping. One time she had even been slapped in the face. She still believed that woman was in denial.

She and Sarah had discussed everything else it seemed, but they hadn't discussed whether either of them was in a relationship. Jessica had been so fascinated by Sarah's woodwork. It was art—beautiful, creative art with wood as the medium. She wanted to get to know her better, and not just for her artistic skills. Jessica wanted to know if her body was as fit under that business suit as she imagined it was. She'd have to think of something fast.

Jessica led the way through O'Hare International like it was her own backyard, practically running in her designer heels. Sarah followed blindly behind her.

"Oh my God, it's cold here." Sarah said as they rushed out the door into the cold Chicago November morning.

Jessica pulled her into a toasty warm, sleek black limo. Jessica nodded at the driver before she pulled the door closed, and he picked up both bags and placed them in the trunk.

Jessica opened the glass between them and Jimmy. A gust of crisp air filled the car as the driver climbed in then wasted no time in getting the car moving. "Thank you so much, Jimmy. We need to stop at 111 South Wacker Drive on the way to the office."

"Yes, ma'am. Welcome home. The traffic isn't too bad. We'll be there in just a few minutes." Jimmy flashed a cheerful smile at her in the mirror.

"How'd you know the address?" Sarah asked.

"I know Chicago."

"This is nice. I'm going to owe you," Sarah said as she rubbed her hand across the black leather seats and looked around at the glistening interior of the luxury vehicle.

Jessica kicked off her heels and relaxed into the seat across from Sarah. Her skirt slid up slightly as she reclined.

"Okay, have dinner with me then," Jessica said quickly before she had time to think about it. *Here goes nothing. Will she slap me while I'm giving her a ride?*

"Excuse me?"

"You said you owe me, right? That's how you pay me back. Come to my home tonight after your meeting, and I'll fix dinner for us."

"And this would be paying you back, how?" Sarah tilted her head and smiled.

"It would be great to have company and I need to know the results of your meeting. Where are you staying tonight?"

"What? Why? I…I'm staying at the Airport Hyatt. I fly out tomorrow at nine, so I'm just heading back out near the airport for the evening."

"And miss the city? Why don't you just stay with me? I live near the lake. It's beautiful, and an easy, quick cab ride from your meeting location. I have plenty of room. It's warm and comfortable, and I can have Jimmy drive you back to the airport in the morning."

"Jessica, seriously, I couldn't impose on you again. You've been too kind already. Besides, you don't really know me."

"Listen, this is my town. I'm being a good hostess. All you have to do to be a good guest is to say yes." Jessica pulled a note pad from the console, scribbled something on it, tore it out, and handed it to Sarah. "Give this to the cab driver when you get done with your meeting. I'm on the twenty-third floor. The number's there on the paper. I'll only be a few minutes in the office this afternoon, so I'll be home when you get there. Jimmy will take me home tonight so I'll bring your bag in with me. You can focus on your meeting knowing all other arrangements are taken care of."

"Umm...I don't know...I mean..." Sarah hesitated.

"It's done. I'll see you this evening."

Sarah started to protest once more, but there was no time. Jimmy pulled over in front of a huge skyscraper. "Ma'am, this is your stop. I'll get your bag for you."

"No, Jimmy. Leave it. We'll drop it at my place this evening." Jessica opened the door and basically pushed Sarah out before Jimmy could get out. "Meyer's offices are on the thirty-sixth floor. I know the receptionist there, Vanessa Summers. She used to work for me. If you need anything, mention my name, and I assure you she will take care of you." Jessica winked at her. "See you this evening."

Sarah was barely upright on the curb when Jessica disappeared behind the door, and the car slid back into traffic.

CHAPTER TWO

S arah steadied herself. *What just happened to me?* She shivered as the damp cold bit at her skin, and it quickly brought her back to reality. She turned to the massive building and walked through the double glass doors into a large entryway with elevators on both sides. Confident that Jessica knew what she was talking about, but not one to leave things to chance, she checked the directory board between the two elevators on the south side to quickly confirm the location of her destination. Sure enough, Meyer Furniture Design had a suite of offices on the thirty-sixth floor. Her stomach tightened and she felt weak as she thought of the consequences of her impending appointment. Building furniture was her passion; selling and big-dog schmoozing was not her thing.

She paused a minute, trying to decide what to do for lunch. The uneasy feeling in her stomach was having an impact on her hunger, but she knew she needed something or she would be useless about halfway through the meeting. Thanks to Jessica and her driver, she still had plenty of time to grab something to eat and run through her design presentation for the millionth time before her meeting started. She had no idea where to go. Maybe there was something in the building and she wouldn't have to go out in that godforsaken cold again. Living in the desert certainly had thinned her blood. She began to scan the directory again for something that sounded like a food court or restaurant.

"Are you looking for something in particular?" A smooth baritone voice sounded from behind her.

She turned to find a distinguished looking man in an expensive suit standing next to the elevator looking over at her. At forty-four, she was in great physical shape. She'd been told often that she looked much younger than she was, and men still followed her with their eyes. Though she wasn't in the least bit interested in them, she was flattered by their attention.

"Well, yes, actually. I was wondering if there was some place to eat in this building."

He approached her and held out his hand. "Joseph Kline. The Townhouse just opened at eleven." He glanced at his watch. "It's a wine bar, and they have great lunches. Just go back out these main doors and enter around the corner." He pointed to the right.

"Thank you, Joseph. That sounds perfect." Sarah took the time to pull her coat on and button it up. She had been rushing since she got off the plane. It would be nice to finally breathe. Maybe she could calm her nerves and relax for a minute. More likely, she would have too much time to think and would make herself even more nervous, but at least she would have a place to sit while doing it.

Joseph took a business card out of his inside jacket pocket. "My pleasure, Ms. ..." He paused, waiting for a name.

"Sarah."

"Sarah...great, good. Here you go." He handed over his card. "I don't know how long you're in town, but call me if I can do anything to help you find a nice place to eat dinner while you're staying in Chicago."

"Oh, thank you." She looked at his card. *Joseph Kline, Attorney at Law.* She smiled and tried not to rush too quickly toward the door. She thought that was weird—flattering, but he was not her type.

She found the restaurant right where Joseph had indicated. It was nice, but as she took in the white linen covering the small tables and the cloth napkins, she knew it wasn't going to be cheap. She was now questioning her decision to upgrade to first-class. Spending that extra money might have been a mistake. But she wouldn't have met Jessica and spent a great morning getting to know her if she hadn't upgraded.

Women like Jessica didn't sit in coach. Also, assuming she actually did stay at Jessica's tonight, she would save a lot on the hotel cost. That seemed a little weird too, but it would be fun to get to know her better. It had been way too long since she had spent time with a beautiful woman—any woman for that matter. Just thinking about it brought up too many tragic images she didn't want to linger on.

But thinking of Jessica caused her stomach to clench with a slight rush of arousal. She wondered if she really had a chance with her. She did ask her to dinner. Sarah questioned herself. Was Jessica interested in her? *Stay focused, Sarah. You need this gig.*

Sarah found a quiet table in the corner and managed to eat a small salad with her laptop open flipping through the same twenty-two slides over and over. She still worried about how the presentation would go, but she did feel a little better since she had time to review and rehearse her briefing. It was twenty minutes before two, and she knew it would only take a few minutes to get to the offices, but she couldn't stand sitting still another minute. She paid and gathered up her things.

Sarah tried to slowly stroll back around the building, but it only took three minutes to get to the elevator. She punched the button marked thirty-six, and in seconds, the doors opened to a large formal reception area with beautifully designed original wood furniture displayed around the room. While the smell of resin and hardwoods was comforting, the room was cold and hard. That just increased the nervous feeling she was fighting.

An attractive young woman with a phone to her ear was sitting at the desk in the center of the room. When she noticed Sarah standing next to the desk, she held up her index finger, made eye contact and smiled. She quickly wrapped up the call. "Yes, Ms. Whitney. Of course. You know I would do anything for you. Actually, she just arrived. Okay. Good-bye."

She looked up at Sarah. "You must be Ms. Jarrett. I'm Vanessa. I'll take you to the conference room." She glanced down at her watch. "You're a bit early. It will be a few minutes before Mr. Meyer is available, but he is very considerate of other people's time so he won't be late. Can I get you some water or coffee?"

"Thanks. Water would be great, but if you could point me to the ladies' room first, I would appreciate it."

"Oh yes, ma'am. Ms. Whitney asked me to take good care of you. Follow me."

Sarah followed her. "Ms. Whitney?"

"Yes, ma'am, of Whitney, Stewart, and Markus. She said you were a friend and wanted me to make sure you had everything you needed. She is so awesome. I worked for her all through high school, and she got me this sweet job. I'm studying at the university, mostly night classes, but Mr. Meyer lets me off for a couple of day classes each week. I want to be an architect just like Ms. Whitney. I would do anything for her. There's no way I could ever pay her back for all she's done for me." She rattled on with her chipper twenty-something attitude.

"Ms. Whitney? Is that Jessica Whitney?" Sarah realized they hadn't exchanged last names.

"Yes, ma'am."

"She is a named partner in an architect firm?"

"She is the firm. Have you seen any of her work?" Vanessa didn't wait for an answer. "The only reason it isn't just Whitney is because she's too humble to take all the credit. She does it all though. Above all, she's an amazing artist, and it shows in every building she designs." Vanessa looked Sarah up and down. "How do you know her?"

"We met this morning on the flight from Phoenix."

"Well, you're lucky. She's a good friend to have around here. Mr. Meyer does a lot of work for her. He often furnishes the offices in the buildings she designs." Vanessa winked.

"She didn't speak to Mr. Meyer, did she?" Sarah wanted to sell more pieces to Meyer. The money would be greatly appreciated, and it would allow her time for her creative work, but she didn't want a handout.

"No, ma'am, but she will if you want her to." Again, Vanessa winked.

"No, no. I was just curious. Thank you, Vanessa."

"Sure, my pleasure. The conference room is just down the hall on the left. I'll get you some water. Oh, and before you leave, stop by my desk. Ms. Whitney asked me to arrange a cab to her condo when you're finished. Have you seen her place? It's incredible and the view of the lake—wow. She invited me to a small office party there once. One day I'll live on the Lake Shore." She stood tall as she walked out.

Sarah headed into the ladies' room. Standing in front of the vanity, she washed her hands and freshened her pale coral lipstick. She couldn't help but think about how small Chicago felt just now. What a coincidence that she had met someone who seemed to know everyone she was meeting with. Sarah brushed her auburn hair and pulled it back again. Her stomach did a couple of back flips. She hated what her nerves could do to her. Her whole life, she always got nervous before giving a briefing, no matter how many she gave.

Looking at her reflection in the mirror, she spoke out loud. "You're good, Sarah. No one builds furniture like you." She smiled at herself. Sometimes the pep talk helped. She made her way to the conference room and opened her computer, but she still had a few minutes. The conference room was massive with enough space for her to walk around trying to settle the sick feeling in the pit of her stomach. There were dark, walnut panels on the walls. The matching conference table was probably twelve feet long. The cost of all that walnut alone was hard for her to imagine. She visualized several projects she could build with that much quality wood. Two huge TV screens hung on the wall in the front of the room, and electronics were everywhere. There was a lot of money in this room. Sarah tried hard to maintain her confidence, but a place like this was intimidating.

Mr. Meyer was on time, but he was alone. She had expected to be presenting to a group of people. Somehow, being alone in the room with the CEO made her even more nervous. She patted her sweaty palms on her pants legs and then went through the entire presentation perfectly, just as she had prepared. She showed him the new pieces she had spent the last six months designing and building. Mr. Meyer nodded and complimented her work throughout the short briefing. When she finished, she exhaled heavily, no longer nervous. She had nailed it.

"Ms. Jarrett, your work is amazing. I'm already seeing returns on the piece we purchased from you this summer, but honestly, my retail line is only a tiny part of my business. I think it would be a waste of your talent to have you continue there. I would like you to move to Chicago and work for me on the commercial contracting side of the business. Your craftsmanship is matched only by your own creativity. I could use a designer like you, someone who knows the wood and loves the craft of building as much as you do. What do you say? I'm sure I can make an offer that would be enticing."

Sarah was so stunned she couldn't say a word. As abruptly as the announcement he just made, Mr. Meyer stood to leave. "Don't answer now. I know you love what you do, so take some time, think about it, and call me back." Sarah's heart sank as she realized he had just turned her down. He wasn't going to buy any of her work. Working in his big business would provide financial stability, but she couldn't leave the work she loved so much. Designing was a big part of it, but getting to build the project, to work with wood every day and seeing the results of her hard work was what she found rewarding. She could never leave the woodshop, not now. She was finally doing what she had always dreamed of.

CHAPTER THREE

Jessica threw open the door of the limo while Jimmy was still pulling up to the curb. "Jimmy, don't bother parking the car. I'll be back down in about thirty minutes. I need you to take me to Whole Foods and the wine store near the condo on the way home."

"Yes, ma'am. Special night?" he teased her.

"Mind your own business, big man," she jabbed back.

Jimmy smiled at her as she rushed off.

As soon as she got off the elevator, she was greeted by her secretary, Mattie, with an extra hot chai latte and a big smile. "We missed you here. Mr. Stewart likes to think he's in charge when you leave, and Mr. Markus walks around like a lost puppy. It's pathetic. They couldn't make it without you."

"I know. I know. They're a mess." She smiled at the thought of her partners here without her. She took the tea and looked questioningly at Mattie. "Did Jimmy text you that I was on the way up?"

"Hey, don't you worry about what Jimmy and I do. Just say thank you, Mattie."

"Thank you, Mattie. Where are those messed up partners of mine?" It was not unusual for her to be cheery with her staff. They were her family, and every one of them worked way too hard because of her, but she was even more cheerful today, and it didn't go unnoticed by Mattie.

"Woo, honey. What happened on that flight to make you so happy? You hate flying, and if you'll excuse my honesty, sometimes you're a bit of a pain in the ass after you return from a long trip."

"No, I won't excuse your honesty, but I will tell you that I have a date." She winked at Mattie. Her office was in the back corner with floor-to-ceiling windows on two sides. She threw everything on the sofa just inside her door and turned back to Mattie.

Mattie grinned from ear to ear. "Way to go! Tell me about her. Where'd you meet? What are you doing? Come on. Give me something."

"No time. I'll tell you tomorrow. Get John and Donald in the conference room. Send in a couple of draftsmen, too. Is Joey here? If not, then Carol and Dan."

"Damn it. Work work work. Yes, Joey is here. Who else do you want, Carol or Dan? They're both here, too." She backed away from Jessica toward the other executives' offices.

"Carol. And can you find me something to eat? Anything? Oh and, Mattie, call Bobby, my wine guy. Have him wrap up six or eight bottles of wine, a variety of his best both red and white. And call Dennis at that seafood restaurant I love and ask him if he can have someone bring over some fresh clams."

"To your condo?"

"Yes. Be sure to tell him I need them before four. He owes me." She grinned.

"Yes, ma'am." Mattie ran to her desk to carry out the tasks.

"Mattie, one more thing. Call that guy from United, what's his name? The guy who helps with my travel arrangements, and tell him to make sure Jean Matthews stays on the first-class staff."

"Curtis Simmons."

"Yes, Curtis. What would I do without you?"

Mattie tilted her head and gave her a cocky smile. Then she jotted the name on her note pad. Jessica was always asking her to call on someone's behalf so she didn't bother to question her.

Jessica walked down the hall to the conference room where her partners sat waiting. Her two draftsmen followed shortly behind her. As soon as she entered, John and Donald started bombarding her with questions about Phoenix.

Jessica passed on the results of her meeting to her partners and staff as quickly as she could while nearly inhaling the Power Bar Mattie had given her. Her associates continued to pepper her with questions.

"Tomorrow, gentlemen. I'll debrief with both of you on everything tomorrow." She got up from the conference table and left them alone.

"What is she doing? I don't think I've ever seen her leave before six." Jessica overheard Donald say as she left.

She hurried through the building, grabbed her coat, and was back to the elevator before anyone else could give her a hard time.

Jimmy was waiting exactly where she had left him, and just as she had predicted, she had only been gone thirty minutes. "Whole Foods please, my good man."

"Forgive me for asking, but has the pretty lady we just dropped off caused you to lose your mind? You just left your office, and it's barely two in the afternoon." Jimmy never pushed it too far, but he loved to joke, and Jessica loved it too, especially when she was so happy.

"Hmm, I can't say."

In minutes, they pulled up to the food store. "Do you want me to go in and help you, ma'am?" Jimmy asked.

Jessica rarely did her own shopping, but she wanted this to be perfect. She wanted to do it all herself. "Nope, I got this. Just wait right here." She jumped out and returned to the car in just a few minutes with two full bags. Jimmy got out quickly and was waiting to take the bags.

"Just get the door for me, please. I'll throw them in the back."

Jimmy held the door and asked, "The wine store?" This was so out of character for her. She was so excited. Her iPad was out, and she was frantically making a list.

They pulled up to the delivery window of the wine store, and the owner was at the window waiting for her. "Ms. Whitney, I have eight different wines here, three red, a blush, and four whites. I know you prefer whites, but your girl said both red and white. Will this work for you?"

"Thank you so much, Bobby. Just what I wanted. Tell your wife I said hello. And put it on my tab."

"Already done. Do you still want your regular delivery next week?"

"Yes, of course. See you then, Bobby." He nodded and waved as Jimmy pulled away.

Jimmy chuckled a little.

"What is your problem?" Jessica tried to sound serious.

"In the ten years since I've been driving for you, I've never seen you like this. You're cute."

"Are you making fun of me?" She smiled up at him, enjoying the feeling that she too, was slightly surprised by. She felt a little out of control, and that was an unfamiliar feeling for her.

"Oh no, ma'am. I would never do that." He smiled back. "I do believe it can all be attributed to the mysterious woman from this morning though."

"Stop laughing at me and wish me luck," she said when she swung open the door as he pulled to a stop in front of her building. "Can you get all this stuff up to me? I'll send the doorman out if you want."

"No, ma'am. I'll be right up."

"Oh, and the luggage, too."

"Yes, ma'am. I've done this a time or two. I think I can manage. Are you worrying?"

She heard the sarcasm in his voice. "No, absolutely not. When have you ever seen me worry?"

"That's just it, ma'am. Pretty much…never." He laughed at her. "Oh, and good luck, Ms. Whitney."

She punched his arm and ran through the door that was already open for her. "Hey, Carl." She greeted her doorman.

"You're home early, ma'am. You just missed Thelma. She left about two minutes ago." Thelma was Jessica's maid. She had been working for Jessica for nearly ten years and knew exactly how she liked everything.

"How does she do that? She always seems to know when I'm going to be home. I would like to see her once in a while." She followed Carl over to his desk. "Is Tyler around? I need him to run an errand for me." Tyler was Carl's fifteen-year-old son. He came by the condo after school each day and made quite a lot of money running errands for the tenants. If it weren't for him and the deli down the street, Jessica probably wouldn't eat most nights.

"I'm sorry, Ms. Whitney. He's still in school. You're never home this early. He should be here in about fifteen minutes though, if you can wait."

She glanced at her Movado, still on Phoenix time. She did the calculations in her head. "Yes, I can wait. That should be fine." She reached in her briefcase and pulled out her wallet. She handed Carl a twenty-dollar bill. "Ask him to go down to Delightful Pastries and pick up a loaf of sourdough bread for me." She thought a minute. "Is that too far for him to walk?"

"No, ma'am. He goes there all the time, and he has his bike so it won't take him long. I'll have him bring you the change."

"No. The rest is for him," she said as she got on the elevator.

"Ms. Whitney, you're driving his prices up with your generosity."

"It's worth it, and he deserves it. He's a very nice young man, and I'm sure you're proud of him," she said as the doors closed in front of her.

❖

When Sarah came out of the conference room, she was greeted by Vanessa's cheery smile. She surely had no idea what had transpired; either that or she assumed it was a good thing. In any case, she told Sarah that everything was taken care of and the cab would be waiting for her downstairs. "If you need anything, you call me," Vanessa said. "Any friend of Ms. Whitney is a friend of mine. Tell her I said hi."

Sarah collected her coat, thanked Vanessa, and took the elevator down to the ground floor with her mind spinning. She was torn between being flattered and being completely disappointed. She had invested a lot in creating those prototypes. The pieces would sell of course, but it would take time. In addition to the large financial investment, she had spent hours designing and building. She had even put off paying customers. She had risked nearly everything, including the cost of the trip. There would be no first-class seat on the way home. *Well, sometimes you roll the dice and win and sometimes you lose.*

When she reached the front door and the cold hit her, she was relieved to see the cab waiting. She glanced at her watch. It was just after four. It was way too early for dinner. The cold, damp wind hit her with a force that nearly knocked her off her feet. She didn't know what else to do so she climbed into the warm cab. This crazy cold weather was as good a reason as any for not accepting Mr. Meyer's offer. She would be glad to get back to her warm desert.

The driver turned to her as she closed the door. "I've been told to take you to 505 North Lake Shore Drive?"

She dug through her briefcase and pulled out the paper Jessica gave her. It had only been a few hours ago, but it seemed like days. With so much preparation and worrying over her presentation, Sarah hadn't had time to think about dinner with Jessica. The thought brought on a whole new set of nerves. Could she spend the evening and night with this beautiful woman and not be tempted to touch her or completely attack her magnificent body? She looked down at the note. "Yes, that's correct. How long is the drive?"

"Fifteen minutes if I have really bad luck with traffic."

"Okay. Any chance we could kill about two hours?" She smiled and laughed. "Kidding. Take me to Lake Shore Drive. Do I sound like I know what I'm talking about?" She laughed again—mostly at herself.

"Oh yeah, you sound like a regular ol' Chicago girl." The slang of his own accent confirmed for her that he was a regular ol' Chicago boy.

As promised, they were there, in front of a huge residential skyscraper at the edge of the lake, in less than fifteen minutes. She could tell it was going to be amazing. She leaned over the seat back. "How much?"

"Already paid—courtesy of Whitney, something and something. Whoever that is. Only thing it means to me is you owe me nothing, and I've been generously taken care of."

Sarah sighed. This was getting to be a little too much. For a moment, she considered just going back to the airport and trying to get a flight out that evening. She could go back to her comforting home, her shop, and also her not so comforting memories and regrets. She shook her head and stepped out of the cab.

Sarah walked up to the front doors of the enormous structure and found that they wouldn't open. She pushed the button on the speaker box. "May I help you?" A deep voice came through clearly.

"I'm here to see Jessica Whitney."

A tall, thin man in a tuxedo opened the door for her. "Good afternoon, ma'am. Ms. Whitney is expecting you." He pointed to the elevator. "Twenty-third floor, ma'am."

Sarah's heels echoed on the highly polished granite floor in the large foyer. Her stomach started the acrobatics act all over again as she approached the elevator. From the looks of this building, Jessica had wealth that had never been more than a fantasy to Sarah. Inside the mirrored elevator, she took a deep breath and pushed the button for Jessica's floor. She looked at her reflection, undid the clip in her hair, and ran her fingers through it. She shrugged. "That's the best you can do."

In just a few seconds, she was on the twenty-third floor, and was walking down the hall to suite 2304, the number Jessica had written on the sheet. She was surprised Jessica was there waiting on her. Named partners didn't usually have the luxury of leaving work at four in the afternoon. She rang the bell next to the door and waited. The door opened and an even more beautiful Jessica stood before her.

Jessica had transformed from the power executive to a casual, relaxed American girl. She wore short, black gym shorts, and a gray, low-cut tank top that revealed just enough cleavage to change the rhythm of Sarah's breathing. She quickly refocused on Jessica's eyes, although they were almost as dangerous. "You look great...and comfortable."

"Thank you. Come in." Jessica held the door. She led Sarah into a wide-open living space elegantly decorated with a less-is-more motif. There was one large painting on the wall next to the small dining table on the far side of the room, and a modular walnut book shelf filled with leather bound books hung over the oversized sofa directly in front of her. The entire north wall facing the lake was floor-to-ceiling windows. Lake Michigan shimmered with the reflection of the sun sneaking through a cloud. The warm orange glow lit the entire room. "You should get comfortable as well. Your bag is in my bedroom." She pointed to the door to the right of the entrance. "Would you like a glass of wine?"

"Ah...yes. Wine sounds great." Sarah followed Jessica into her modern, stainless steel and glass kitchen. It was small but functional.

"Red or white?" she yelled, not realizing Sarah was right behind her until she nearly knocked her over when she spun around. "Oh, I'm sorry. Please feel at home here. You should go ahead and change."

"White." She tried to get out of Jessica's way in the small kitchen not made for two people. "Well, I didn't really expect to do anything tonight. I was just planning to go back to the hotel and chill. I don't have anything but an old T-shirt and pajama pants. I'm fine like this. I might kick off my shoes though if you don't mind."

Jessica poured two glasses of white wine. "That sounds more comfortable—the T-shirt and pajamas I mean. Go put them on." She paused and looked over at Sarah. "Sorry. I didn't mean for that to sound like an order, but seriously, you should go change. I'm basically wearing pj's myself. I know your day has been as long as mine, so instead of chilling in a stuffy hotel room, chill here." Jessica winked at her and handed Sarah a glass of wine. "This is a Washington State Riesling. If you don't like it, I have plenty of other selections. This is my favorite, but I've been accused of having a sweet wine palate."

"Um, well, okay. I just didn't want to be presumptuous and run around in my pajamas in your home." She turned to the door Jessica had indicated earlier. "I'll be right back."

Sarah found her bag sitting on a short rack in the corner. She stopped and looked around the room. She felt a surge of excitement as she ran her hand across the fluffy comforter on the king-sized bed. The room was painted a pale green with one wall a dark blue. It was small, and the large bed in the center took up most of the space. Everything in it whispered high class and money. Two large pieces of art hung on the wall above the bed. She knew nothing of art, but she did know those pictures were beautiful, and they had to be worth thousands. The grain pattern in the exotic wood used throughout the matching bedroom set was stunning and unfamiliar to Sarah. She examined it closely, but she was still unsure what it was.

Even with all the expensive decorations, the room was still inviting. As she examined the decorations, she realized she was standing in the only bedroom. She had taken in the relatively spacious condo in one glance when she walked in the door. She paced back and forth in front of the bed as she contemplated the sleeping arrangements. She soon gave up on the problem and stripped off her suit.

Sarah walked out in her favorite sleep shirt, a faded, too tight, Air Force T-shirt, and a pair of slightly baggy pajama pants hanging low on her hips.

"Hmm, better." Jessica smiled and scanned her top to bottom.

"Not my most fashionable attire, but you're right; it's much more comfortable. Thank you." Sarah was a little embarrassed at the way Jessica looked at her. She wondered if things were heating up too fast. She didn't know if she was ready to open herself up to someone again. At least with Jessica, when she left in the morning she could be sure she would never see her again. Maybe sharing a purely physical moment with someone so incredibly gorgeous might feel damn good. Maybe she could allow herself a meaningless sexual encounter with someone way out of her league. She wouldn't have any expectations of her. Perhaps Jessica just needed to find out what it was like being with an average girl.

Jessica handed her wine back and guided her toward the windows. "Check out my view. This makes the hassles of living in the city totally worth it."

"Jessica, I couldn't help but notice in your fantastic home here that you have only one bedroom. I'm thinking perhaps it would be more comfortable for you if I went back to the hotel tonight instead of imposing on you." She could feel the attraction she had for Jessica in her body every time she looked at her. But when she imagined lying in that bed with her, Sarah felt a wave of dread. Where could she go in this small place in the middle of the night if the feelings of loss and sadness that sometimes seemed just below the surface overcame her with this virtual stranger? By big city condo standards, it was probably large, but Sarah lived in the West where a small house would fit two of these condos inside it.

"Just enjoy the view. We'll worry about sleeping arrangements later."

"Ah...okay." Sarah walked behind her to the windows, eyeing the couch for its potential as a bed. The lights in the living space were dim so she could see out across the lake as the sun faded. The orange sky had turned to a deep violet, and the city lights reflected off the still lake in an assortment of reds, oranges, and yellows. As beautiful as it was, she couldn't help but be distracted by the muscles on Jessica's exposed back and shoulders. She had a great body, and not touching that silky skin required some effort. She took a big sip of wine. This was going to be an interesting night.

"It is an incredible view. I'm not sure I could ever feel comfortable in a city like this, but I can see why you like it here," Sarah said, forcing herself to focus.

"So how did it go today?" Jessica turned slightly to face Sarah putting her only inches from her face.

Sarah felt a surge and eased back ever so slightly to breathe and break the effect. "Not great—it was basically a wasted trip." She explained what happened with Mr. Meyer and how the day ended.

"He said that? After you did all that work? Wow. That's so disappointing. Will you be able to sell them?"

"Yeah, eventually." Sarah exhaled, forcing out the frustrations of her day. "It wasn't what I was expecting. I mean it's flattering that he wants me to work for him, but I just couldn't leave my business. It's small and not very profitable, but I've worked too long to get the one thing I've wanted my whole life. I just wouldn't fit in here." Sarah smiled and looked out the window at the lake and city below her.

"Would you like me to call him? He values my business, and I'm sure I could convince him to reconsider."

"No! No, absolutely not!" That came out sharper than she had intended. "Sorry. It…it…just…it is what it is. I took a risk, which is a stretch for me, so that's good. It just didn't work out this time. I don't want the big architecture firm owner to get me work. If my designs don't speak for themselves, well, so be it. I have a clientele. I might build a lot of standard furniture pieces without a lot of artist style going into it, but I get to work with wood every day. That's what I want. And yes, I'll sell the pieces. If I'm lucky, I might even make more money than Meyer would have paid me. There's an art dealer in Phoenix who loves to show my work. He'll be thrilled that I have so many pieces at once. I can usually only bring him one or two pieces at a time. It'll just take a while. I don't need a handout." Her voice rose again slightly. Sometimes pride was her biggest enemy or maybe her favorite mask. She changed the subject. "You didn't tell me you were a named partner with connections all over this town."

"I'm sorry. I didn't mean to imply that you needed my help. I…I just…" Jessica clearly didn't know what to say. "It never came up. My family has been a part of the Chicago business scene for generations, mostly lawyers and underhanded politicians." She laughed. "I broke away. I'm a bit of a black sheep. I was to take over my dad's firm. He didn't get the son he wanted, and his only daughter does her own thing. Anyway, I'm sorry."

Jessica looked at the darkening sky and then back to Sarah with her eyebrows raised and her head tilted a bit to one side. "Of course your work can sell itself." She reached her hand out to almost touch Sarah's wrist. "He didn't want to just buy the product. He wanted the product designer all for himself."

"You're right. It's an amazing opportunity, and that's why I wasn't upset. I'm out some time and some funds, but for anyone else it would have been the chance of a lifetime. It's just not for me—not at this time of my life." Sarah relaxed again seeing that she had verbally punched too hard. Jessica was just trying to help. "Thanks for having Vanessa take care of me. She was very sweet and adores you. And the cab, you didn't need to do that." Sarah took a deep breath and let it out then smiled at Jessica over the edge of her wine glass before she put it to her lips.

"Vanessa is sweet isn't she? She's so young, and I'm afraid she's slightly infatuated with the lesbian executive. Anyway, I'll make sure she gets a position in the firm when she finishes school if she wants it. I just have to draw some clear boundary lines for her." Jessica's face flushed red.

Jessica had just confirmed what Sarah had figured out on her own with the growing sexual tension in the room. It was now out in the open with Jessica's confessions of her sexuality. This was a date—a little unconventional, a first date in pajamas, but it was a date.

CHAPTER FOUR

Jessica had been having trouble keeping herself from staring at Sarah's amazing body from the minute she invited her into her condo, but Sarah made the challenge almost impossible when she came out in that sexy, tight T-shirt. Jessica saw that Sarah wasn't wearing a bra. It was subtle, but the curves of her small, shapely breasts were accentuated in that shirt. An image flashed in her head of what it would be like to pull it over her head and caress those soft curves. Sarah had a natural beauty that required no artificial enhancements. Jessica could tell that while she was confident and sure of herself, Sarah had no idea how beautiful she was, and that made her even more beautiful.

Jessica returned her focus to Sarah when she started talking again. "There was one interesting thing that happened to me today."

"Really? I want to hear about it, but first, are you starving? Should I start dinner or would you like to sit in here and tell the story?"

"No. Actually, I'm not too hungry yet. You?"

"Let's sit." Jessica motioned to the oversized sectional. They both sat and turned to face each other, their knees only inches apart. Jessica sensed the heat of Sarah's body so near and wanted to edge closer so they were touching, but she was still working up the nerve. She couldn't be quite that forward. "So tell me what happened."

Sarah adjusted herself on the sofa and relayed every detail of the Joseph Kline experience. "That's weird, right? Rich, handsome men don't just walk up to people like me and give them their business card."

"Sarah, seriously. Have you seen yourself? That is not weird at all. You're beautiful. I'm just surprised you only have one business card to show for your day." Jessica finally reached out and gently touched Sarah's leg. "You know he's disappointed that you haven't called him yet."

Sarah shivered beneath Jessica's light touch. Her face flushed a bright shade of red, but that didn't stop her from reaching for Jessica's hand. She returned the small show of affection as the heat exchanged between them intensified.

Jessica slumped a bit when Sarah pulled away quickly. She wondered if things were moving too fast for her. Jessica was being drawn in by Sarah's sweet, poised personality and gorgeous body, but maybe Sarah didn't feel the same way, or maybe she was just uncomfortable at how rapidly things were heating up.

Jessica worried that she got her answer when Sarah quickly changed the subject. "You know, I'm kind of hungry now that I think about it."

"Dinner…yes. How do you feel about linguini in clam sauce, with a salad and some awesome fresh bread from my favorite bakery?" Jessica was determined to slow down and not push her away.

"Sounds great. How can I help?" Sarah raised her glass as she stood. "Besides, we need more wine."

Sarah followed Jessica back into the tiny kitchen. Jessica refilled their wine glasses. "How do you feel about cutting a few vegetables for the salad?"

"I think I can handle that. I'm really not too handy in the kitchen," Sarah admitted and took a big gulp of wine. "But I'm good at cutting things; haven't cut any of my own fingers off yet."

"That's good," Jessica said as they both grinned at each other.

Jessica pulled out a knife and a cutting board before clearing a small space on the counter. She pulled a bag of veggies and some spinach leaves out of her refrigerator. "Here you go." She went to work on draining the noodles and left Sarah to her task.

"Hey, don't cut yourself with that knife," Jessica teased Sarah when she looked over and saw Sarah manhandling the vegetables. "Aren't you supposed to be good with sharp tools?" Jessica noticed Sarah had finished her second glass of wine and hoped it would help her relax a little.

Sarah was smiling down at the work she was doing and took a deep breath, letting her shoulders drop.

"This is not a power tool, and these tomatoes don't have quite the same texture as hardwood. Trust me, you can put any power tool in my hand, and I'm a magician." She looked over at Jessica and caught her eye and winked. "But most of these kitchen items are like foreign objects to me."

"Just don't ask me to help you with a saw. I could do some serious damage," Jessica said.

They were both clearly relaxing, and sideways glances turned into brief direct looks into each other's eyes.

Sarah popped a piece of tomato into her mouth. Jessica had an urge to kiss the lips that were smiling and moist with tomato juice, wiping the plump lower lip with her finger.

They made it through dinner preparation with a few casual accidental, but more frequently purposeful, contacts in the tiny space. At one point, they bumped hips, both going for the sink at the same time. She was no longer nervous and wanted to let Sarah know how much she'd like to wrap her legs around her sexy body.

❖

A long time ago, Cheryl had told Sarah that if she died first to find someone who could cook for her. It was a joke. They had been standing in the kitchen looking at a lopsided birthday cake that Sarah had made for Cheryl, both of them laughing. Sarah had picked up the cake and pretended to throw it in Cheryl's face, but instead put it close to her own face and took a big bite out of it. That was Cheryl's thirty-fourth birthday. Neither one of them had any clue how few birthdays were left for them.

"That was delicious. Even with all your kidding, I didn't mess anything up," Sarah said. "I can't seem to make even a simple birthday cake. They all turn out looking like a condemned building."

"It was good, wasn't it? It was just that my ridiculously wonderful cooking skills overcame all of your shortfalls." Jessica winked at her. "I'm just sayin'."

"Whatever." Sarah smiled. "Well, I am good at cleanup. That was always my job."

"Your job? Who assigned you to cleanup detail?"

Sarah paused, realizing she had said too much. Right now, she didn't want to share any of her real life regardless of how much she enjoyed Jessica's company. "Oh, nothing. I'll get the dishes." Sarah jumped up from the table with plates in hand heading for the kitchen.

"Did I say something wrong?" Jessica followed with the salad bowls and glasses.

"No. I ah…is there any more wine?"

Sarah was grateful that Jessica didn't push the personal questions. "Yes, of course. Would you like the same one or something different?"

"I liked what we've been drinking. It's very good, but you choose."

Jessica pulled out a bottle while Sarah leaned over her to reach for a dishcloth to wipe off the table. As she did, she bumped Jessica's shoulder. Jessica rose quickly, and Sarah found herself staring right at the smooth, dark curves of Jessica's cleavage. A pulse of desire rushed through Sarah as she stared at the swell of Jessica's breasts.

"I caught you!" Jessica winked and smiled at her.

Sarah flushed red but quickly made eye contact. "Oh my God! I'm so embarrassed. I'm an idiot."

"Don't be silly." Jessica flashed that amazing smile and lightly touched Sarah's waist. "I put them there for you." Sarah felt goose bumps rise on her skin from Jessica's light touch.

The increased tension between them had reached a climax. Sarah stared up at Jessica. Jessica's lips hovered only inches from hers. Her desire to kiss Jessica was overwhelming. Sarah moved in closer before she could think. Jessica met her halfway and slid her arms around Sarah's neck pulling her closer. Their lips met, and they both exhaled heavily. Jessica moaned softly. Jessica's warm, soft lips consumed her, the kiss gentle at first.

Jessica welcomed the kiss. She opened her mouth, inviting Sarah inside. When Sarah felt Jessica's breasts and her belly and her thighs press into hers, a shiver ran through her entire body. Sarah couldn't stifle a low, throaty moan. She felt her knees weaken as Jessica kissed her with a hunger she wasn't prepared for. She matched it, sliding her hands up Jessica's bare shoulders. Sarah pulled her closer and stroked her neck as her tongue traced the surface of Jessica's lips. She groaned again as Jessica's tongue slipped past her lips.

The closeness felt so good, and for that moment, she forgot all the reasons why it had been so long since she had let anyone be so intimate with her. Her heart pounded heavily in her chest as she felt Jessica's tongue tangle with hers. Jessica clung to her, keeping their bodies pressed tightly together. Sarah moved her hands freely across Jessica's back, then lower, cupping her tight, round buttocks. She was overwhelmed by the fierceness of their kiss. After so many years of being alone, Sarah felt a passion again. She struggled to remain standing as she returned each kiss with equal enthusiasm, delighting in the arousal she felt. It had been so long since she had experienced that rush of desire. Sarah pulled at Jessica's shirt. She wanted it off.

Jessica took Sarah's hand and led her through the short hall to her bedroom. Sarah's pulse was pounding so loudly that she felt sure it was audible. As Jessica pushed her bedroom door open with her foot, she moved in for another kiss. Breathing heavily, she leaned back and searched Sarah's face. Jessica pulled her in for another kiss. Sarah knew they both felt the same way and wanted the same thing. Jessica finally released Sarah's face and reached down for the bottom of her own shirt. She took a deep breath and slowly pulled the shirt over her head.

Sarah sucked in air and felt her stomach clench with the swift rush of arousal. For the first time tonight, Sarah allowed herself to stare freely at Jessica's stunning body. She was so toned and fit, and her dark skin highlighted every muscle. Sarah finally focused on the black lacy lingerie that still covered her round, full breasts. As Sarah eagerly looked on, Jessica unfastened her bra and let it fall to the floor. Sarah's hungry gaze traveled over Jessica's naked upper body. Her heart pounded heavily and her stomach did one slow flip.

"Jessica, you're so beautiful," Sarah whispered and pulled off her own shirt exposing her naked breasts. She never thought she could experience this excitement again, and the unmistakable flood of desire that swelled within her was both thrilling and terrifying.

Jessica looked down at Sarah's breasts. Sarah looked up, meeting Jessica's eyes. She saw her desire reflected back at her. Sarah moved toward Jessica and touched her thin waist. She put the other hand gently to Jessica's face and pulled her toward her. Feeling Jessica's firm body beneath her touch sent chills across her body, and she moaned as they kissed. Jessica didn't hesitate, her mouth opened and her tongue met Sarah's.

Jessica's soft lips felt so good. Jessica gasped as Sarah moved her hands up to cup her breasts. Sarah caressed them, enjoying the feel of the soft curves in her hands. Sarah rubbed her fingers across Jessica's nipples, the sensitive skin turned hard from her touch.

Jessica caressed Sarah's bare back and shoulders, pulling her closer. Her hands moved to Sarah's hips. Jessica pulled away briefly and gulped in deep breaths. Sarah paused to take in air as well. Jessica's touch was both gentle and confident, like the warm water of a shallow stream. Sarah's body reacted to her every move. Sarah slipped her fingers to the waistband of Jessica's shorts, and she pushed them down with her panties in one fluid motion. Jessica stepped out of them, and she was standing there completely nude.

Sarah pushed her pj's down, and for a brief second, they stood exposed before each other. Jessica pulled Sarah to the bed and yanked at the comforter revealing cream-colored silk sheets. She lay across the bed and reached for Sarah, pulling her down to her. Sarah covered Jessica, and she felt the smooth softness of her skin against her own. As Jessica slid her hands across Sarah's back, Sarah nudged her thighs apart. Jessica's hips slid apart and rose to meet Sarah's body as she pressed into her.

"You. Feel. So. Good," Jessica murmured, kissing her between words.

"You have no idea," Sarah said against her lips. Sarah moved her hands down Jessica's body, and she felt Jessica tremble as she slipped her hand between Jessica's smooth thighs. Jessica bent her knee to open herself up to Sarah's sweet touch, urging Sarah to take her. Encouraged by Jessica's movement, Sarah reacted, and she could feel the rush of her own juices.

Sarah moved her fingers through Jessica's slick folds, her hips jerking when her fingers rubbed lightly across her clit. Jessica pulled Sarah's mouth to hers, panting when Sarah sucked her tongue inside at the same instant her fingers filled her. Jessica pulled her mouth away. She inhaled deeply and her hips moved against Sarah in a natural rhythm. Sarah lowered her head and her tongue moved across Jessica's rock hard nipples, first one, then the other. Sarah heard Jessica moan again as she covered her breast, sucking a nipple into her mouth. It was absolutely incredible. Jessica's body rocked with Sarah's rhythm, and the pace of her breathing increased. Finally, a low scream escaped from her mouth, and Sarah felt her body explode around her. As Jessica's body went limp beneath hers,

Sarah moved down Jessica's body, both hands spreading her thighs again.

Jessica began to protest. "Wait I…wait…not this soon."

Jessica breathed deeply as Sarah ignored her and settled her mouth over her clit. She sucked it hard, rubbing her tongue against it. Jessica's hands squeezed the sheets, and her hips rocked against Sarah's face. Jessica was amazing. She reacted to Sarah's every touch. Sarah loved her taste. She wanted it to last forever, but she felt Jessica's body responding. For the second time in minutes, she brought Jessica to an intense orgasm. She nearly exploded herself from Jessica's screams of pleasure and the pressure of Jessica's legs squeezed tight around her. Sarah rose slowly from the grip of Jessica's thighs. Jessica lay still on the bed and took in short quick breaths. Sarah moved her hands slowly now and softly caressed Jessica's beautiful, soft body.

Sarah whispered, "How do you feel?"

"Incredible…" Her breathing finally slowed. "Absolutely incredible."

Sarah kissed her shoulder and moved slowly up to her ear. "Incredible is good."

Jessica gained her composure quickly. She rolled toward Sarah, who was nestled next to her. She moved her mouth to Sarah's ear. Her breath caught as Jessica's lips moved against her neck. She felt Jessica's soft lips lingering behind her ear.

Jessica cupped her breasts, and Sarah relished in the pleasure of hands on her sensitive flesh. Sarah's nipples hardened against Jessica's palms, and she moaned. Jessica rose slightly and looked at Sarah. "Jessica, that feels so good." Sarah leaned back, offering herself to Jessica.

"Beautiful," she whispered as her mouth enveloped one of Sarah's breasts. Sarah ran her fingers through Jessica's thick, wavy hair and held her close. She moaned softly as Jessica teased her nipple with her tongue. As she moved her mouth over Sarah's breasts, she also moved her fingers down her body touching every inch of her soft skin. Jessica lifted her head again, meeting Sarah's eyes. Her eyes were glowing with arousal and desire; her lips slightly parted, her breasts rising and falling with each quick breath she took. Jessica kissed and nuzzled Sarah's warm flesh as she moved down her body.

Sarah still had her fingers entangled in her hair, and she pushed, gently urging Jessica downward. Sarah whimpered as Jessica reached her stomach and subtly shifted her hips. Sarah wanted her to hurry, but Jessica made her wait as she slowed down, teasing Sarah with her tongue. Jessica ran her hands down Sarah's legs and then up again. Sarah felt the wetness between her thighs.

"Oh my God, Jessica. Please just fuck me," Sarah said in a breathy voice as Jessica kissed the inside of her thigh, still teasing. Jessica parted Sarah's thighs, cupped her butt, and groaned with pleasure as she settled her mouth over Sarah. She slid her tongue across Sarah's swollen clit. Sarah raised her hips and moved slowly against Jessica's mouth.

"Jess…oh, yes," Sarah breathed. As her orgasm threatened, Jessica shifted, thrusting two fingers deep inside Sarah as her tongue flicked across her clit, faster and faster. Sarah felt herself building and building until finally, she couldn't hold back any longer. Her body simply exploded, bursting with pure pleasure, and a scream escaped from her mouth. She jerked against Jessica's face before slowly sinking back against the pillows.

"How was that?" Jessica smiled as her fingers slipped slowly from Sarah, and she rested her head against Sarah's thigh.

Sarah pulled Jessica up beside her, and they kissed softly, slowly caressing. Sarah tasted herself on Jessica's moist lips. "That was amazing." Sarah sighed. "It's been a while. Thank you."

"Thank you. I've been fantasizing about running my hands across your body since I watched you walk in front of me down the Jetway in Phoenix this morning. Being with you was better than even my wildest imagination." Jessica moved closer to kiss Sarah's neck and climbed on top of her. Jessica moved down Sarah's body again with wet kisses across her breasts and then her stomach. She moved her hand between their bodies and found Sarah's clit.

Sarah reached for her hand and stopped her, saying between heavy breaths, "Jess, oh my...stop...stop for a second. If we're going to do this all night, first I need to set an alarm and then make arrangements to get to the airport tomorrow. After another round, I'm going to be completely unable to move."

"Are you always the sensible one?" Jessica panted with desire. "That's all taken care of. I told you already. Jimmy will take you to the airport. The service will call an hour before he's scheduled to arrive, and he's never late. Relax." She pushed Sarah back against the pillows and picked up where she had left off, trailing kisses across her stomach. She moved over Sarah's clit for the second time tonight, but it wouldn't be the last.

Sarah relaxed and enjoyed Jessica's soft touch. For now, there were no boundaries between them or their urges.

CHAPTER FIVE

Sarah jerked awake at the sound of the phone buzzing. Jessica's head was on her chest, and their legs were tangled with the sheet partly covering them. She didn't quite remember falling asleep. It couldn't have been but a couple of hours ago.

"Jess." She nudged her lightly. Sometime during the night, Jessica's name had just been too long, and she had shortened it to Jess. "Jess...the phone."

"It can't be time to get up." She reached for the phone. "Thank you so much, Sophie," she answered with no greeting. "Yes. I'm sure I'm awake. See you in a couple of hours. Please ask Mattie to bring in some bagels from the shop on the corner. Okay, see you."

She rolled on top of Sarah. She kissed her and pressed her bare breasts against Sarah's. Sarah felt the familiar rush and reacted by opening her lips to receive Jessica's tongue, and their quick breathing matched. Jessica cupped her breasts and moved down with kisses on her neck. Sarah arched up to meet her mouth. Jessica sucked her nipple, still sore from so much touching and sucking throughout the night. Sarah flinched from the tenderness.

"Jess, I've got to get up and get showered or I'll miss my flight. As much as I would love to lie here with you all day, I have to get back home and back to work."

Jessica caught her eye. "Okay. You're right. If we start again, I don't know that I could stop. Shower with me? I'll be good. I promise."

The shower was a marvelous combination of botanical soap, shampoo perfumes, and the silky touch of hands on wet skin. They had sex, and just as Jessica had promised, she was good.

They continued to flirt and kiss while tripping over each other in the small bathroom, giving themselves only a few minutes to dress. Sarah barely had time to get her luggage packed before there was a knock on Jessica's door.

"Who's that at this hour?" Sarah asked.

"Jimmy."

"Your driver comes to your door?"

"He's getting your bag. He brought it up here yesterday. He knew he would need to come get it." Jessica was dressed in one of her tailored business suits, and her still-damp hair was starting to tighten up into loose waves.

"Good morning, ma'am. Is your guest ready to go to the airport?"

"Jimmy, meet Ms. Jarrett. Sarah, Jimmy."

Sarah nodded politely.

"Nice to meet you, ma'am."

Jessica pointed to the bag Sarah had just rolled into the front room. "Take Ms. Jarrett's bag down and meet her in front of the building in about ten minutes. Oh, and call me when you're on your way back. I'll be down to meet you."

"Yes, ma'am." The big man moved past Jessica and picked up the bag as if it were empty and slipped out the door.

"Thank you, Jess. You didn't have to give up your driver. I could have called a cab," Sarah said.

"Really, it's no big deal." Jessica moved toward Sarah and wrapped her arms around her. "Last night was amazing. Thank you." She kissed her lightly, and Sarah pushed into her as their lips met.

"It was," Sarah said before she kissed her again. "I gotta get going."

"I would like to see you again. I'll be in Phoenix in a couple of weeks."

"Yeah, sure," Sarah said and moved away from her. She was starting to create a distance before she even got out the door.

"Are you okay?"

"Yeah," Sarah snapped too curtly. "I just need to get going. I hate airports and flying."

"So can I call you?"

"Yeah, of course. Call me." Sarah kissed her and moved swiftly out the door.

In the elevator, she began to process what had happened. That was the last thing she expected this trip to be about. Jessica was a raw experience of intimacy. Sarah kept reliving the passionate moments from the night before—the tenderness and ease they felt with each other—but she wanted none of this. She refused to feel anything. Not now…not yet. It was too early. She didn't know if she ever wanted to have feelings for another woman. These were the thoughts running through her head as she reached the ground floor where the limo sat waiting. Jimmy was standing by the car tapping on his cell phone. When he saw her coming, he slipped the phone in his pocket and opened the door for her. "Ms. Jarrett, I'll have you at the airport in thirty minutes."

"Thank you, Jimmy. May I call you that?"

"Yes, ma'am. That's my name." Jimmy flashed her a big teddy bear smile. "You can close the window if you'd like. The button is there to your right."

"Oh. I'm not used to riding in a car like this. I think I prefer to leave it open if you don't mind." Sarah made eye contact with him in the mirror.

"I don't mind at all. Ms. Whitney never closes it either. She always wants to talk to me. She is the most generous person I've ever met. I would do anything for that woman."

"You're not the first person I've heard say that about Ms. Whitney. She does seem to make an incredible impression on people."

"Yeah, everyone loves her. When I first started working for her I was in a bit of a financial situation. My newborn daughter had a lot of medical bills. She was premature and had to stay in the hospital for several weeks. She's almost eleven now. Wow, how time flies. Anyway, I would have lost everything I owned trying to pay those bills. She paid them all. I insisted on paying her back every penny, but Ms. Whitney continued to give me excessive bonuses every time I made a payment to her. I think she believed she was fooling me, but I've finally realized I'd just have to play this little game with money. I know I'll never be able to pay her back financially, but instead I'll be the most loyal driver and bodyguard a woman could ever have."

"Jess needs a bodyguard?" Sarah asked.

"No, probably not, but she has one."

"I'm sure she appreciates your loyalty far more than the money," Sarah said. "Sometimes money makes you question your friends, so having loyalty that you can count on is probably very comforting."

Jimmy pulled up to the curb in front of the United Airlines departure doors within seconds of the time he had quoted. He was ready to open the door for her before she could gather her things, and he had her bag in his hand. "I'll carry this over to baggage drop-off for you."

"I'm going to carry it on with me. Thank you, Jimmy." She tried to give him a tip.

He refused, and she was slightly embarrassed. "Oh no, ma'am. You're Ms. Whitney's friend. It was obvious to me this morning that she likes you a lot. I'll see you, ma'am." He quickly moved away from her.

❖

Jimmy called at about eight thirty and told Jessica he was ten minutes away. She would be in the office by nine. It was later than her normal arrival, but she hoped no one would notice. She figured she couldn't hide the exhaustion, but it was worth it.

When she arrived at work, she rushed through the reception area where Mattie was on the phone, but of course she spotted her. She passed by the draftsmen in the center offices to her office in the back of the suite that was Whitney, Stewart, and Markus. Why hadn't she put her office in the front? She smiled at herself. It was because her office was the best.

Jessica's life was the firm, and mostly that was all she wanted, but sometimes she felt like she was missing something. She turned on her computer and pulled up the files for the Phoenix project. She had a couple of hours before she started with the meetings that would fill the rest of her day. The guys in Phoenix were nitpicking mostly. She hated that. She took great pride in her work. She knew it was art, and this project was no different.

It had been years since she had dedicated herself completely to a project. Jessica had so much to do to run the business that she didn't get to do what she loved. She realized that last spring when she was sitting in a meeting desperately wishing she was somewhere else—anywhere else. She definitely didn't want her father to know that her life wasn't exactly what she wanted.

Daddy wasn't happy with her, but Gramps had loved her artistic abilities. He had encouraged her all the way. In the end, despite her dad's best efforts to keep it from happening, Gramps had set her up for success. In his will, he left her the suite of offices, and a large bank account that she was to use exclusively for starting her own firm.

She hadn't spoken to her dad in nearly three years after her last attempt to reconcile with him. She was an only child and her mother, who had basically disowned her when she told her she was a lesbian, had passed away about ten years ago. Her work was her family, and she had never felt like she needed anything else. The people at the firm took care of each other, and they loved her. Jessica was generous with her success, and she was the matriarch of her little community, her firm.

There was one problem with her close community; they always knew each other's business. Mostly, there was nothing going on in Jessica's life so there wasn't much to talk about, but it had escaped no one that she left early yesterday and was not the first one in the office this morning.

She even felt the eyes of her partners looking at her now as she struggled to focus on the project. The glass offices were beautiful and modern when they put them in, but it certainly contributed to their tiny little community gossip. She dug deep down to energize herself to concentrate on the Phoenix building, but on top of being exhausted, although she rarely slept much, she was also distracted.

She kept seeing Sarah's face close to hers, her slightly wide set eyes, the lips parted and smiling like someone who had found an oasis in the desert. She thought of writing her a note, a real snail mail card, poetic with a line like, "I want to be your oasis in the desert." *Was that too cheesy? Should she confess to her that she had never had more than one orgasm in a night with any other woman? Was that too...?*

She heard her name called, not Jess, but Jessica. She looked up to see the other faces in the room waiting for her to say something.

"I'm sorry," she said. "What was the question?"

CHAPTER SIX

Sarah arrived back in Phoenix with her head spinning. She had again hoped to sleep on the flight home. She'd never had trouble sleeping on a flight before, even in coach, but she couldn't stop her mind as she went back and forth from basking in the amazing experience she just had with Jessica, to the unbelievably heavy feeling of guilt for enjoying herself so much.

On her drive home from the airport, Sarah stopped to pick up Benny from the kennel. Benny was her brindle, female boxer. She had been a constant companion for almost ten years. Benny was ecstatic when the kennel owner brought her out to Sarah. Her little nub bounced around at the end of her bum, and she shifted around on all four feet barely stopping herself from running out to the truck. Sarah put her in the backseat of the truck, and she stuck her nose between the front seats, pushing her head against Sarah's arm for the whole trip home.

It was still early when she got back to the house. She made a ham and cheese sandwich and grabbed the phone along with her customer list. It was time to solicit some work. The bills would not stop coming just because she didn't succeed with Meyer.

Three of her loyal clients had agreed to wait until after she finished with her work on the prototypes. She'd call them first. Then she had to call David to see if he had room for any of the pieces in his gallery, otherwise she wouldn't have any space in the shop to work or she would have to bring all the pieces in the house and trip over them.

No more stalling. It was time to call Patricia. She had only been home for a few hours, and Patricia had already left two voice messages and texted a half a dozen times. She, like Sarah, had been sure this was the break she needed to get in a better financial position. She always seemed to be able to pay all her bills, thanks in part to her military retirement check, but getting that contract with Meyer sure would have eased the pressure and allowed her more time to create, but it wasn't meant to be. She just couldn't accept his offer. There was no leaving her workshop to spend all day at a desk in a big city. She'd call Mr. Meyer back tomorrow.

Sarah picked up her phone and pressed the button for Patricia.

"Welcome back. Tell me all about it." Patricia always answered her phone with questions or demands.

"He didn't want to buy the furniture," Sarah said matter-of-factly.

"Are you kidding me? What do you mean? That was part of the deal when you sold him your dry bar design. He can't do that. You spent months getting those pieces ready."

"I know, Patti. It's a crap deal, but he wanted me to work for him in Chicago. I'm sure he thinks that's a better offer than just buying my furniture."

"You're right. That's total crap. Did you tell him he could stick his job?"

Sarah laughed at her. "No, he asked me to think about it. I'm sure in his world no one in their right mind would turn him down, but I could never leave..." Sarah paused. "There's so much here I don't want to leave behind."

"I know, honey. And Chris and I wouldn't let you leave anyway. We'd tie you down," Patricia said. "Hey, get over here. I have a new wine I want to try, and Chris is working late."

"I'd love to, but I have three customers that I've put off forever. I called everyone, and they're ready for me to get back to work. I need to put some numbers together tonight and go pick up lumber tomorrow. How about you guys come over next week for steak? I'll fire up the grill."

"We love your steaks—especially Christine. She's always after me to have you show me how to make them. Okay, it's a deal. Promise me you won't work too hard, and you'll be careful in the shop."

"I'm always careful in the shop. Come by on Tuesday about six. It's supposed to be nice, so I'll burn some scraps in the fire pit. Bring your wine!"

"Are you okay, Sarah? I know you were counting on this."

"I'm good. I'll make it up. Don't worry. I'm fine. See you in a few days." As she thought about all the bills that would be arriving in the next couple of weeks, she wondered if she was trying to convince Patricia or herself.

"Okay, sweetie. Call if you need anything."

"Right. Love ya." Sarah clicked off.

Now it was time to see if Joe would extend her a bit more credit for the new projects. She knew he would, but she hated to ask. Joe had backed her every step of the way since she opened the business part-time when she was still in the Air Force. He knew how good she was and never once treated her differently, despite the fact that she was one of the few women who ever entered his hardwood store.

❖

Sarah glanced at her watch. It was almost five thirty. Patricia and Christine would arrive in a half hour, and she still hadn't showered. She had been in the shop for nearly ten hours a day for the last four days straight. The mahogany platform bed was almost ready for its first coat of finish. Sarah made herself stop and quickly swept the shop. In just a few minutes, she was out of the shower and French-braiding her hair when the doorbell rang. She scrambled to finish the braid as she ran to the door with Benny bounding behind, her toenails clicking on the ceramic tiles.

"Hey, ladies." They all exchanged hugs. "I just got out of the shop. I don't have anything ready, but it won't take a second. I did have the foresight to put the steaks in the marinade before I went to the shop this morning."

"You haven't eaten all day, have you?" Christine said as she handed her a bowl of salad.

"I had breakfast, and I think I ate a protein bar sometime during the day." She tilted her head. "Hmm, well, I had planned to. Does that count?"

Christine frowned at her. "Sarah, seriously!" She turned to Patricia. "Patti, will you talk to this woman? She won't listen to me. I'm going to get this wine open." Christine made her way to the kitchen. "Well, at least I love your steaks."

Patricia and Sarah followed behind her with Benny close on their heels taking turns leaning on each of them soliciting some attention.

"You're only saying that because you know I can't make anything else." Sarah ignored the scolding. She knew they worried about her, but at least she was doing better. There had been more than a few days when Patricia came over after ten p.m. and found her still in the shop so exhausted she was dangerously close to causing an accident or so high on chemical fumes she was about to pass out.

"At least what you do, you do very well," Christine teased her.

"What are you working on?" Patricia asked and took the wine bottle from Christine, as she struggled with removing the cork. "You get the wine glasses." She pushed Christine out of the way. They were quite familiar with Sarah's kitchen. Christine gave Patricia a dirty look and went to the cabinet to get the glasses while Sarah got the steaks out of the refrigerator.

"Bring that stuff out here. It's finally cool enough to sit outside," Sarah said as she headed for the back patio. The view was not great because it looked right at the plain brown stucco wall of her workshop building behind her house, but it was well shaded, and the November temperatures had finally cooled things off.

Patricia and Christine met her on the patio and settled into the teak patio furniture Sarah built years ago.

Sarah got the grill ready and put the steaks on. She looked over at Patricia. "You asked what I'm building. Remember Matt Jackson? He ordered a bunch of pieces from me last year. He had me build his daughter a full bedroom set from mahogany, minus the bed. Now I'm building the bed for him. It's a custom platform bed. He wants to give it to her for Christmas so the timing is perfect." Sarah glanced at Christine. "How are you doing? Patricia tells me you've been really busy."

"Yeah, I've been crazy busy at work. They're really messing with me because they know how badly I want to be a partner. I'm one of three attorneys being considered. It seems like I've had twice as many cases as anyone else, and most of them are court cases. It's consuming. We're hoping to get a break soon and get away for a week or so during the first part of December, but Patti has two new clients with full houses to decorate so we somehow have to coordinate all our work efforts." Christine paused a minute, clearly done with that topic. "Sarah, I'm sorry about the gig with Meyer. Patti told me. I thought sure it was a done deal."

"Yeah, thanks. You know how it is. I'm meant to work for a living. It's a good thing I love it." She turned the steaks and the grill sizzled.

"I told her not to mention that. I'll get the salad. Christine, be good, will you?" Patricia bent to kiss her while poking her in the ribs.

"Hey, grab the plates and silverware I put on the counter while you're in there," Sarah yelled behind her.

Sarah served up the steaks, and Christine was the first to dig in. "Delicious as always. Other than the bad news, how was the trip?"

Sarah smiled. "I met this gorgeous woman on the flight to Chicago."

Patricia looked up abruptly. "What? You didn't tell me that. What was she like?"

"Well, she's rich, very rich. She's a named partner in an architecture firm, and from what I can tell, it's a pretty major firm. She was very nice. I really enjoyed talking to her. She had a limo pick her up, and she gave me a ride to my meeting."

"Really? More please," Patricia pried as she cut off her next piece of steak.

After Patricia and Christine pulled and pulled, finally Sarah told them everything including that she had spent the night with Jessica. She left out a few of the better details.

"Sarah, that's great," Christine said. "Are you going to see her again?"

"I don't know. Probably not. I mean really, where would it go? She's out of my league, and besides, I'm not ready."

Christine started to speak again, but Patricia stopped her with a kick to the shin.

"Ow, damnit, Patti. Stop that." She frowned at her.

"Sarah, it's great that you had a nice time with a woman. That's good, right? That's good." She looked over at Christine.

"She's right. I'm glad you enjoyed yourself. You deserve it," Christine said.

"So what's next week look like for you?" Patricia quickly changed the subject.

Dinner was a feast of juicy steaks and familiar friends. Sarah often forgot how much she loved having them over. She had learned to defend her feelings by working almost nonstop, but it helped to feel human once in a while. No matter how much time had passed by, spending time with Patricia and Christine made her think of Cheryl, and sometimes that was too hard to take.

It was nearly eleven when they left, and Benny had already taken up her spot by the door waiting for Cheryl to come home. Almost three years had passed, and Benny still believed Cheryl would be home at eleven thirty when her shift ended. Sarah wished she could explain to Benny that Cheryl was never coming home. After she hugged Patricia and Christine and sent them home, she sat on the floor and wrapped herself around her dog. It was a familiar position, one she had taken up countless times in the first year after Cheryl was killed.

Slowly, she had managed to stay beside Benny less and less, but tonight she missed Cheryl so badly. She felt guilty for enjoying herself with a woman she barely knew, and wanting to see Jessica again. Sarah laid her head on Benny's soft fur, and tears began to fall as she drifted off, struggling with the intense pain of the past and the present fear of caring for someone else. It was an internal battle that left very little room for anything else.

Chapter Seven

Sarah twitched as her phone rang. It had been a particularly long and hot day in the shop, and she had fallen into bed as soon as she had climbed out of the shower. She usually forced herself to stay awake until Cheryl made it home from her mid-shift, but most of the time she fell asleep with her computer on her lap in her old recliner, the one Cheryl continually tried to get her to throw out. Cheryl teased her all the time about not being a night person, but when Cheryl came home, she would kiss Sarah lightly to wake her up, and lead her slowly back to their bedroom where often, even when they were both exhausted, they would make love.

Sarah grabbed the phone as she glanced at the clock: 12:04. "What is it?" She struggled to get the words out as her voice caught.

"Sarah, it's Mark." Mark was Cheryl's partner at the Phoenix narcotics division. They had been assigned together for the last six years. Cheryl had followed Sarah to Phoenix on her last Air Force assignment to Luke Air Force Base. Sarah knew Cheryl thought he was a great partner, and she trusted him completely.

Given the hour and the fact that Mark was calling, not Cheryl, Sarah knew it was bad. "Mark, what is it?" She finally found her voice. "Where's Cheryl? What's going on...what? Mark tell me. Tell me what happened, Mark. Mark—"

"Sarah, stop and shut up!" His harsh tone caused her to stop and gain some composure. "Now just listen to me," Mark said calmly and slowly. "Get up and get your clothes on. Two uniforms are on their way to pick you up. They're going to bring you to the hospital where I'll be waiting for you."

"I'll drive. I'm fine. I'll be right there. Is she all right?" Sarah knew how dangerous Cheryl's job was. Phoenix had one of the most active narcotics units in the country.

"Sarah, get dressed and walk out the front door. The uniforms will be there, and they'll bring you in with sirens. It will be faster and safer. Do you hear me?" The cop in him was coming through loud and clear.

"Okay. But just tell me, is she okay?"

"Just get here soon. I don't know what to say right now." He cut off the line.

Sarah pulled on a pair of jeans and a T-shirt. She grabbed a pair of socks and shoes and ran to the front of the house nearly tripping over Benny as she ran. The uniforms were standing next to their patrol car in front of her house. She ran toward them. Her legs nearly gave out as she approached. The patrolman closest to her caught her arm. "Ma'am, I'm going to get you to St. Luke's. Get in. We'll be there in seven minutes." He opened the door for her, and she collapsed in the backseat.

They arrived with sirens blaring. Sarah was opening the door before he could get the car stopped. She sprinted barefoot into the emergency room. Mark was at the door when she reached them. She saw his face and knew it was bad. She nearly dropped to the floor. For the second time that night, someone kept her from falling to the ground. Mark caught her and held her so tight it was almost painful. She dropped her shoes and socks on the floor and never saw them again.

"Sarah, I'm...oh, Sarah." Mark struggled to hold back tears. "I'm so sorry."

Somehow, while Mark was losing his strength, Sarah found some. "Where is she, Mark? Is she dead?"

"Follow me." Mark led her through the ER lobby, where a short female doctor approached her.

"Ma'am, I'm Dr. Stark." She looked at Mark. "Is she next of kin?"

"I'm her wife! Tell me what's going on." She started to yell, but forced herself to calm down. "Doctor, please, we've been together nearly fifteen years. Please take me to her."

Dr. Stark didn't hesitate. "She's in here. I'm so sorry. Ms. Johnson suffered from a gunshot wound to the head, and she has shown no signs of brain activity since we resuscitated her about two hours ago."

Sarah followed behind trying to make sense of what the doctor just said as they approached a small patient room. She looked around the room at all the machines connected to her beautiful wife. A bandage covered most of the left side of her face. The tube coming out of her mouth looked so foreign. Sarah moved as if in slow motion, taking in her surroundings. She finally spoke so softly they barely heard her. "She has a DNR."

"We know that now, but when she came in we had no medical records for her. We performed all life saving measures," the doctor said, almost apologetically.

Sarah turned to Mark. "Mark, you knew." She was so calm, showing no emotion until one tear rolled down her face.

"Sarah, I'm sorry. She was shot entering the building at the scene." Mark broke down, and his voice cracked as he continued. "I called it in, and they came for her while we were still in pursuit. I couldn't leave the scene. They were undermanned and outgunned. I couldn't leave. I'm sorry. I wasn't here with her. They shouldn't have sent us there. They were waiting for us. We were fucking ambushed." He wiped his face on his sleeve.

Sarah froze at the end of the bed, and the doctor and Mark both looked at her. Mark took her arm as she wobbled a little unsteady on her feet.

"Mark, call her mom." Sarah gave out directions.

"What…you…me? Sarah you should call her."

"Please, just do it," she begged. "She won't want to hear from me, and this has to be taken care of. You know Cheryl wouldn't want to be like this." Sarah crossed the room to Cheryl's bedside and took her hand.

"Cheryl, damn you!" Sarah's voice was high and squeaky. "You were supposed to be careful." She climbed in the bed beside her and began to sob.

Sarah was still in the bed with Cheryl, staring blankly at the right side of her face when the doctor returned to the room. From where she lay, she couldn't see the damaged side of Cheryl's face, and she could almost make herself believe that Cheryl was just sleeping. Mark stayed with her and was sitting in the short leather chair beside them. It made him look like a little boy so low in the seat.

"Sarah," Dr. Stark spoke softly.

Sarah looked at her.

"Mrs. Johnson just called back and told me that we should honor her daughter's request and turn off the machines."

Sarah nodded in agreement. "Do you do it now?"

"Yes."

Sarah turned to Mark. "Would you mind leaving us alone?"

Mark stood and touched Sarah's hand and then touched Cheryl's. He turned and hurried out the door as tears rolled down his cheek.

"Sarah, I'm going to turn off this machine, and she could live for hours or she could pass within minutes. I'll leave you when I'm done, okay?"

Sarah nodded.

Dr. Stark turned off the ventilator and left. Almost immediately, the heart monitor's beeps came slower and slower and finally made a continuous squeal.

Sarah jerked awake with the buzzing sound echoing in her head. Benny raised her head from her night watch duties to look at her. Sarah had a terrible kink in her neck. It was nearly two in the morning. She hadn't relived that nightmare in months. She knew she couldn't blame Jessica. It was her own guilt and feelings of loss that brought back the dream, but the guilt was due to the time she had shared with Jessica. She got up and made some tea. Patricia would be proud of her. A year ago, she would have gone back out to the shop and worked herself to exhaustion. Benny normally stayed on her night patrol until Sarah got up and made her go outside in the morning, but tonight she followed Sarah into the kitchen and sat with her while she drank her tea. Maybe Benny was healing too, or maybe she knew Sarah needed her beside her.

CHAPTER EIGHT

Mattie stood in Jessica's office entryway and tapped on the doorframe. She was holding an envelope. Jessica grunted and waved her hand to motion her in the room, but she didn't stop typing.

"Jessica, I'm heading out. Here are your tickets, hotel information, and meeting times and locations." She set the envelope on Jessica's desk. "I put everything on your calendar, and Jimmy has the rental car information. He and Sam will pick you up in the morning, and Sam will bring the limo back. You're all set." Mattie turned to leave. "I'll see you in a few weeks."

Jessica finally stopped typing and looked up. "Thank you so much, Mattie. Is there anything here I need to sign before I go?" She pointed to a stack of papers on her desk. "I won't get through all this tonight."

Mattie returned and pulled out one form. "If you sign this, I can go ahead and restock office supplies while you're gone. I'd have to explain every purchase before Mr. Markus would sign it."

"I thought you just signed my name to those purchase sheets?" Jessica laughed. She knew her partners were paranoid about spending money. She spun the sheet around and signed it without looking. "What else am I forgetting?" she asked as she handed the sheet to Mattie and motioned for her to sit down.

"We got it. Don't worry, hon." Mattie dropped into the comfortable chair in front of Jessica's desk. "Are you going to see your friend while you're out there?"

Jessica leaned back in her leather executive chair. It almost consumed her. "I guess not." She bit into her lower lip and gently shook her head. "I sent an e-mail a few days ago letting her know I was coming out, but I didn't get a response."

"You should call her. Maybe she has a new e-mail address or maybe she's not as crazy about keeping up with her tech devices like some people I know." Mattie pointed a finger at Jessica.

"We didn't exchange phone numbers. I had to get her e-mail from Vanessa over at Meyer's office. I don't want to push too hard. If she doesn't want to see me, then I'll go there, get my job done, and get back home." Jessica did her best to pretend she didn't care.

"You liked her. You thought she liked you. It's okay to be disappointed."

"Thanks, Mattie. You should get out of here. It's late. Go home. I'll see you in a few weeks."

"Okay, my dear. Call me if you need anything." Mattie patted her hand before she left her alone.

Jessica finished up some paperwork and finally packed her computer and briefcase around nine thirty. Then she phoned Jimmy.

"Good evening, Ms. Whitney." His low, deep voice sounded awake, as if he had been waiting for her call.

It made Jessica happy to hear his strong positive voice when she was so exhausted. "Do you think you might be able to give a tired woman a lift home?"

"It would be my pleasure. I'll be out front by the time you get to the door."

Jessica locked the suite of offices and got on the elevator. When the doors opened on the ground floor, she saw Jimmy through the glass doors standing next to the car, waiting to open the door as soon as she was outside.

"Thank you so much." She smiled weakly and climbed in. They rode in silence during the short drive to her condo.

"Sam and I will be here at seven. Sleep well, ma'am." Jimmy said over the top of the car as she walked to her building.

"You too, Jimmy. See you tomorrow."

Jessica had worked until after nine or ten most days since she had spent the night with Sarah. She had been busy preparing for the trip and arranging for day-to-day operations to continue while she was out of town. Even though she had only spent one night with her, she thought of Sarah a lot when she was in her condo by herself. She knew that was why she had worked so much over the past couple of weeks.

She poured herself a glass of wine and looked through the items Thelma had set out for her to put in her carry-on bag. In one quick glance, she knew that Thelma had considered everything. She quickly put it all in the bag that was also set out for her. Jessica stripped off her suit and pulled on an old T-shirt and shorts. Then she poured another glass of wine and went to the front room to unwind before trying to get some sleep.

Jessica reclined on her couch and looked across the water. She realized how disappointed she was that Sarah hadn't called or responded to her e-mail. It had been five days since she sent it and nothing. Sarah had made it clear when she left that she really didn't want to see her again, but Jessica was hoping she was wrong. She finally got up and put her wine glass in the sink and climbed into her bed.

❖

Sarah had worked non-stop for two weeks. She spent every waking hour in the shop and finished the platform bed ahead of schedule. Every debt she had was due, including her house and truck payment, which would consume nearly all the profit from the bed. She would be paid in full for the work today, and she would turn it around and pay as many bills as she could. She was going to have to ask Joe to take far less than she had promised him. It was going to take her a while to get back on her feet. She made some major cuts in her budget, but there were still more bills than money.

If she focused on the jobs she had lined up, she could make ends meet and have a good start on making up for her loss. However, she would have to get some more work for the winter soon, and there would be no breaks. If she could sell some of those prototype pieces that David was showing for her, that would take the pressure off, but she realized that could take months. Her creditors wouldn't wait. For now, she had to get the bed delivered and get the first payment, so she could start on the next project.

Sarah called Chad, her neighbor, to help her load the bed and assist with the delivery. He was always willing to help out for a little extra cash. The two of them loaded it up on her trailer and had it delivered before noon. She went directly to her bank with a nice paycheck. It was a start. She loved designing and building art, but the custom furniture projects were sometimes even more satisfying when the customer saw the work for the first time. Matt Jackson had seen her work before. He was great to work for because he was always so impressed and complimentary of her work. It felt good to be appreciated for her talents. He was particularly pleased today. He knew his daughter would love it. Additionally, he gave her hope for a new major project. He had money, and his wife was in need of a present for their anniversary in March.

Sarah returned from the bank and sat at her computer to pay bills. The heavy burden of owing money was one she wanted to shed as quickly as possible. It was the first time she had sat at her computer in several days. She had been so focused on getting the bed finished. It had consumed her, not because it was difficult and required a great deal of thought, but because she didn't want to think about anything else. Every time she began to think about the amazing evening she shared with Jessica, she felt guilty.

But when she saw Jessica's name in her e-mail queue she smiled, happy to see it there. She opened it before she even looked at any of the others. It was sent almost a week ago. She wondered how Jessica got her e-mail address, but then she remembered Jessica had connections with Meyer's secretary. She opened the e-mail.

Hey, beautiful. I hope you made it home safely. Thank you so much for the wonderful evening. I'll be arriving in Phoenix on the 20th, and I would really like to see you again. Call me if you would like to have dinner (312) 821-9664. Please call. Yours, Jess

Today was the twentieth. Sarah was worried she was too late. Jessica probably thought she didn't want to see her, but she was so excited about the e-mail she could hardly keep from running to her phone. She picked it up and pushed in the numbers, but she stopped short of hitting send. What was she thinking? Jessica could only be a short-term thing. It would only end in more pain and that damn guilt.

The internal struggle continued, but maybe a short-term affair would be okay. Maybe she didn't have to feel guilty if she was just having some good sex with a hot chick. Even as she processed all of it, she knew it sounded so much simpler than it actually was. She really liked Jessica. She wanted to see her, to be with her again, to talk to her, and of course more great sex would be appreciated.

This time she would be the host. This was her city. But she had no money, at least not enough available right now to take someone like Jessica to dinner. She could have her over and make her specialty. She might even be able to bribe Patricia for her spinach and strawberry salad. She pushed send.

After the second ring, she heard Jessica's sweet voice. "Hello."

"Hey, it's Sarah. I just got your e-mail. I've been really busy, and I haven't even been on my computer for days. Sorry it's the last minute." She didn't take a breath. "Are you still interested in dinner?"

"Sarah, it's great to hear your voice. I'm just glad you called. I was convinced you didn't want to see me again. Of course, yes. Let's do dinner. Give me your address, and I'll have Jimmy come get you. Let's go casual. I really like the Citizen Public House. It's downtown. Do you know it? I can't wait to see you. I was going to get tickets to a show and—"

"No, Jess. That's not how it's going to be," Sarah interrupted and laughed.

"You want to go someplace else?"

"No. In the words of a beautiful woman I met in Chicago, 'This is my town.' I'm being a good hostess. All you have to do is say yes to be a good guest."

Jessica laughed. "Oh, I see. Okay, yes! What am I agreeing to?"

"I'm going to give you my address, and Jimmy is going to drive you here. Tell him I'll have something ready for him as well. And I'm going to fix dinner for you tomorrow night."

"Sarah, I remember you weren't all that into cooking. You don't have to do that. We can go out somewhere," Jessica said.

"Are you worried about my lack of skills in the kitchen?" She heard Jessica's wispy laugh. "You have no idea what I can do with a grill. I'll make you the best margarita you've ever had, and if you want to see a show, well, I have a great selection of nineties hopelessly romantic movies. Lame, I know. Maybe we can think of something else to do."

"Interesting. I didn't take you for a hopeless romantic kind of girl, but I'm interested in the something else," Jessica said.

"Um, yeah so my address…" Sarah told Jessica her address and started to describe how to get to her house, but Jessica stopped her.

"Apparently, you know my driver quite well if you are planning to feed him, so you know he'll get me there by the best and quickest route."

"Of course he will. Besides, it's easy."

"Thank you for calling, Sarah. I'm really looking forward to seeing you. Is seven okay?"

"Yes. Seven is perfect. I'll see you tomorrow," Sarah said and clicked off.

❖

Jessica tossed her phone on the end table and looked out the big balcony windows at the desert mountains in the distance. She didn't really see a thing. She was too excited to take in a view. Feeling like a little kid waiting for a trip to the amusement park, she couldn't wait to see Sarah again. She had spent the whole day convincing herself it was better that she hadn't called, but now she realized just how much she had been lying to herself.

Prior to Sarah's call, Jimmy had just left her in the luxurious Presidential Suite at the Ritz-Carlton, and she was dreading the three or four weeks in front of her. It was the same stuffy, unwelcoming suite she had stayed in when she was here a few weeks ago, but she no longer minded the cold, oppressive feel, because Sarah called. Sarah wanted to see her. Jessica plopped herself down on the stiff sofa, allowing herself a minute to enjoy the thought of spending time with Sarah.

Sarah didn't work at all even though she knew she should be getting ahead on the next project. Instead she spent the day cleaning the house, the dog, and the shop. She hadn't cleaned in way too long—at least not a really good cleaning. As she dusted off the surfaces she began to put pictures of her and Cheryl in drawers. She hadn't realized how many they had—so many memories.

At noon, Sarah rushed around the house looking for her phone when she remembered she needed to call Patricia. She hoped it wasn't too late or too much to ask at the last minute.

"Good afternoon. What're you doing?" Patricia answered.

"Hello, my dearest and most wonderful friend," Sarah said in a sweet, syrupy voice.

"Oh, it's like that, is it? What do you want?"

"I need a last minute favor. Please tell me if it's too much to ask."

"Sarah, stop it. What do you need?"

"Can you please make me some of your spinach and strawberry salad? Please?" Sarah begged.

"You just had it the other night. I know you don't like it that much."

"I'm having a date over for dinner, and you know the only thing I can do is steaks on the grill."

"You have a date? Who?" Patricia paused. "I'm sorry. Of course I can. When do you need it?"

"Ah, well...tonight."

"Oh my gosh, Sarah. A little more notice would be appreciated. I'll have to leave now to get the stuff," Patricia squealed into the phone.

"I'm sorry. I can pick everything up at the store if you don't have time."

"Are you kidding? No, you won't. I know how you shop. I'd have to go back and get all the stuff you forgot. I'll be over in a couple of hours."

"Patti, I owe you big time," Sarah said, realizing she could never pay Patricia back if she lived a million years. "It's Jessica, the girl from Chicago, by the way." Sarah clicked off.

Sarah continued preparing while she waited on Patricia. She had gone to her favorite meat market first thing and had the butcher pick out the best rib eye cuts, and they had been marinating all day. She set up the back patio for dinner. Even the margaritas were mixed. She'd been rushing around wildly giving a whole new meaning to multi-tasking, but it was after six, and she hadn't been in the shower yet. She was still wrestling with Benny in the bath. She didn't mind the bath, but Sarah wanted her to be dry when Jessica arrived. She should've bathed her earlier, but she didn't, so it was blow-dryer time. Benny absolutely hated the blow-dryer. She kept trying to crawl behind the bathroom door to get away from the air blowing on her.

When she finished with Benny, she quickly got in the shower. In minutes, she was using the blow-dryer on her own hair. Knowing Jimmy wouldn't be late, she finished putting on a little bit of eye makeup just as the bell rang. Benny barked only once. Sarah took one quick glance in the mirror. "Not too bad," she said.

Benny ran to the door and sat looking up at it. Sarah followed right behind her and flipped on her iPad and selected random play. It was connected to internal speakers around the house, and she was happy to be surrounded by Nelly Furtado's "Forca." She looked down at Benny. "Sit and stay! You hear me? I know it's hard for you to believe, but not everyone loves dogs." Benny tilted her head as if she were taking in all the words.

Sarah opened the door, and Jessica stood before her with a bottle of wine in one hand. She was wearing snug designer jeans emphasizing every sexy curve, and a red linen blouse that showed off her thin waist. She looked fantastic.

"Hi," Jessica said.

Sarah was a little awkward leaning in to kiss her cheek while Jessica turned to kiss her lips. "Um…come in." Sarah motioned for her to enter. Benny was doing a little jig, trying hard to keep her bum on the floor while her nub of a tail spun in a tiny circle. "This is Benny."

"May I pet her?" Jessica leaned down but hesitated. "She looks like she could be mean."

"Of course you can pet her. She's going to bust if you don't." Sarah looked at Benny. "Don't you dare jump!" Benny rose and did her standard move of pushing into Jessica's legs to encourage her to keep up the petting.

"She's really pretty good. Once the newness of having you here wears off she won't bother you, but if you don't like dogs I can put her in the spare room. She won't like it, but she'll understand. I've told her not all of my two legged friends like her."

"Don't be silly. She's great, and I love dogs." Jessica continued to scratch Benny's ears. "She's very pretty and her fur is surprisingly soft."

She smiled at Jessica. "She's my best friend and spends the entire day in the shop with me. I worry about her ears with the machines. I've tried to make her stay in the house, but she is so pathetic when I come in. She walks around like she's being punished. So she has a blanket out there, and she loves to be wherever I am."

"I was a little scared of her when I first walked in. I bet she's a good guard dog."

"She is, but she reads my reactions well. She knows when someone is welcome and when someone isn't. It's comforting to have her. Oh! I just remembered—did Jimmy already leave?" Sarah moved in the direction of the kitchen to get the plate she had warming in the oven.

"He did actually. He was grateful for the offer, but no one has ever done that before, and I think he felt a little awkward. He told me he already ate, which could be true." Jessica shrugged. "Anyway, he said to tell you thanks very much."

"That's too bad. Well, okay." Sarah turned back toward Jessica. "What does he do while he waits for you?"

"Well, normally, he finds somewhere to hang out and read. He reads everything and anything and is on a classics kick right now. He always wants to discuss them with me, but as far as classics go, if it's not *Pride and Prejudice*, I'm lost. Anyway, tonight I told him to go back to the hotel, but I promised I'd call him as soon as I wanted him to come and get me. It's only about fifteen minutes away."

Sarah winked at her. "Is that in case you don't need a ride?"

Jessica smiled that spectacular smile that melted Sarah every time. "A girl can hope."

"Hmm." Sarah returned a smile. "Are you thirsty for my very dangerous margarita?"

"That sounds great." Jessica glanced around, "Sarah, you made everything in here, didn't you? This wood is beautiful." Jessica ran her fingers over the top of the cherry sofa table. "What is it about wood that makes you want to touch it?"

"It's seductive, isn't it?" Sarah smiled. She understood more than anyone the appeal of wood. It kept her in business. "I started building when we moved in here while I was still on active duty. Woodworking was a hobby back then. Now, after five years, I'm running out of room to put things." She ran her fingers across the top of the table until they met Jessica's and touched lightly. "Don't look too closely at some of the pieces in here. I was still perfecting my craft, and there are more than a few flaws."

"Are you kidding me? I'm sure they are only flaws that you can see, because you're a crazy OCD perfectionist," Jessica joked and tried poking Sarah in the ribs.

"I'll take that as a compliment." Sarah moved toward the kitchen. "Drink? I see you brought wine. Would you prefer a glass of wine?"

"No, no, I've been excited about margaritas all day. I just wanted to bring this for you. What should I do with it?"

Sarah took the bottle and thanked her with a light kiss and smiled. "It's good to see you."

"And it is good to see you. I was a little worried that you had walked out of my life forever. I had such a nice time with you in Chicago."

"Me too." Sarah meant it and standing there with Jessica right then, she had forgotten all the reasons she had questioned it. "Salt and lime?"

"Yes, please."

Sarah prepared the margaritas and motioned Jessica to the back door. "I'll bring these out. Everything is set up on the patio. I'd really like to sit outside if you don't mind. It's so rare we can enjoy the outdoors here, so when it cools off I take every advantage."

"No, I don't mind. I'm enjoying the warm weather." Jessica headed to the door with Benny leading the way. "Can she go out?"

"Try to stop her." Sarah looked down at Benny who was already showing her approval. It didn't hurt that Jessica had barely stopped petting her since she arrived. "Yeah. She'll stay in the yard. When she's done wandering around and sniffing, she'll lie down under the table. She figured out early on if she wanted to get to hang around with us, she had to be good."

Sarah finished making the drinks and headed out. She found Jessica wandering around the backyard. Sarah caught up to her and handed her a glass.

Jessica took a long drink. "This is great. I can see it has the potential to be very dangerous." Jessica enjoyed another sip. "I assume this is your shop."

"It is. Not much to look at from the outside. It's just a big ol' building that most of my neighbors don't like. I tried to blend it in with the look of the neighborhood, but it's still a bit out of place." Sarah looked over at the massive structure that was her life.

"Can I see it?" Jessica asked.

"You want to?" Sarah loved to show off her shop.

"I can't wait. I love power tools." Jessica grinned and interlocked her arm with Sarah's.

Sarah opened the door. The smell of resin and the unique scent of fresh cut mahogany was overwhelming.

"What is that amazing smell? It smells like leather in here," Jessica said.

"That would be mahogany." Sarah was so used to it she barely noticed. She picked up a small cut-off, sniffed it, and handed it to Jessica.

Jessica inhaled deeply, holding the piece under her nose. "I love it and the grain is beautiful."

"A woman after my own heart." Sarah smiled and walked around the shop. It was so perfectly organized and clean that it almost shined. She had spent half the day cleaning and putting everything in its assigned space. If the truth be known, she spent more time cleaning the shop than she did the house. She was a little uptight about her shop so most everything stayed in its place, but now and then after rushing through a big project like the bed she had just finished, things could get out of hand.

"Wow, Sarah this is wonderful." Jessica walked around the shop brushing her fingers across the shiny equipment making her way to Sarah's favorite tool, her full-sized cabinet-maker's table saw. "This saw is huge!"

Sarah beamed. "Thanks. I'm pretty proud of my shop. It has taken a long time to get here, but this is why I could never take a desk job in Chicago." She spun around. "Who could leave all this?" Sarah held her arms out and laughed.

Jessica walked over to Sarah leaning against her workbench. She pulled her close and embraced her for the first time tonight.

"I've wanted to hold you since the moment you opened the door standing there all sexy in your baggy jeans."

Sarah returned the hug that she had wanted as well. When she opened the door and saw Jessica, she had felt like a teenager on her first date not knowing what to do with herself.

Jessica lingered in the hug and finally backed up to look at Sarah. "You have a great place here, and you should be proud. I completely understand why you wouldn't want to leave."

"Yeah, it's pretty great." They both looked around the large workspace. "Are you hungry?" Sarah asked and Benny bumped her leg rather hard. "Not you."

"Yes, actually I am a little hungry." Jessica spun the ice around in her empty glass. "And I could use another one of these, but I can see I'd better slow down or I'll be under the table while you're eating."

"It just occurred to me, and I could be really screwed," Sarah said hesitantly, realizing she had failed to ask before she bought the meat. "You eat red meat, right?" Sarah tried not to show her panic as she waited for Jessica to respond. She had no idea what she would feed her if she said no.

Jessica laughed. "I can see it would be a lot of fun to tease you and tell you I don't, but I'm one of the few women in my generation who has never given up meat. I love it too much, and I really do eat pretty well—you know the old-fashioned all-in-moderation concept. It has served me well and still allows me to enjoy the things I love so much. What can I do to help?"

"Not a thing. Just sit and relax."

Sarah started up the grill and Jessica sat at the table next to her.

"What have you been up to since I last saw you?" Jessica asked.

"Working. I pretty much hit the ground running when I got back. That's why I didn't see your e-mail until last night. Truthfully, I wasn't sure how to feel about you and me. But really, I was busy. And my art dealer agreed to put my pieces in his gallery."

"That's great news. I'm sure they'll sell in no time."

"I hope so. What about you?"

"Same, really. I spent the last two weeks getting ready to come back out here to finish up the deal. I made several design changes and had to answer thousands of questions about the style. That's why I'm planning on being here for the next couple of weeks while they get started on the building."

"So you'll be here for the holidays?" Sarah asked.

"Yeah, actually, I guess I will. And then I'll be back and forth to monitor the project."

Sarah couldn't help but think of some other benefits they might enjoy with Jessica spending so much time in Phoenix.

While Sarah prepared the steaks at the grill, Jessica sat next to her and patted Benny. She asked questions about places to go in Phoenix and the surrounding beauty of the Southwest. By the time they sat down to eat, they both sighed, relaxed, and took a minute to look into each other's eyes. Pushing the salad bowl toward Jessica, Sarah said, "I have to confess that my friend Patricia made the salad."

Jessica smiled while putting a piece of steak in her mouth. She closed her eyes and said, "Sarah, this is the best steak I've ever had. I'm serious. What did you do to it?" She cut off another bite.

"Don't sound so surprised. You were afraid I was going to poison you, weren't you?" Sarah said. "It's my secret marinade. My friends Patricia and Christine are always trying to get me to use it on chicken, but I have the heat and timing down perfectly for the steak. I'm a little concerned about taking the leap to chicken. I'm getting a little tired of it myself, but it's the one thing I knew I wouldn't screw up, and I had to impress you somehow."

"Hmm, if I recall, you've impressed me plenty already." Jessica winked at her.

They finished the meal and found themselves tripping over each other in the kitchen once again. Sarah stopped and grabbed Jessica around the waist and spun her around to face her. She looked briefly into her eyes, and with no words, pulled her to her and kissed her deeply. They breathed heavily, releasing the tension that had been building. Sarah moved her tongue past Jessica's parted lips and explored. She felt the immediate rush of pleasure through her body and the familiar feeling of arousal between her thighs.

"I'd like you to follow me to my bedroom, but before we get there I want you to call Jimmy and tell him to pick you up for your meetings in the morning," Sarah spoke softly in Jessica's ear.

Jessica kissed Sarah with hunger and turned to do as she was instructed. Before heading to her bedroom, Sarah grabbed the candles she had forgotten to light at dinner. She dashed around her room, lighting the candles and pulling her blankets back. She was fueled by her desire to be with Jessica.

Jessica finished making arrangements with Jimmy and walked to the back of the house. "I love all the space you have, and you've decorated it so elegantly." It was painted in several hues of beige. Heavy brown curtains blocked any evidence of outside light. There was a slight hint of vanilla from the candles and the soft glow created a warm and romantic effect. Jessica moved over to the cherry platform bed.

Sarah watched her walk across the room. She was so beautiful, and the way she carried herself was such a turn-on. She was sure of herself, but not arrogant. Sarah took in every curve, the shape of her. She moved like a sleek wild animal. Sarah stopped only inches from Jessica and looked into her eyes.

A warm rush passed through her and a pressure built in her chest. She was falling for this woman. She hardly knew her, but damn, she was amazing, and being with her was so easy and felt so good. She pushed the thought from her head and moved in closer, their lips only inches apart. Sarah paused there, not touching her. She felt Jessica's warm breath on her cheek. Jessica moved in to close the space, but Sarah backed away. Jessica looked at her and frowned. Sarah smiled, placed her hands on Jessica's hips, and pulled her close.

Jessica parted her lips and allowed Sarah to move her tongue into her mouth. She greeted it with her own. Sarah moved with her slowly and deliberately, increasing the intimacy with every touch. A shiver ran down her spine and a stirring rushed through her stomach. Sarah wanted her now, but this felt so warm and delicious.

Sarah sucked Jessica's tongue into her mouth as she moved her hands across Jessica's slim waist and up to her full breasts. She felt them moving up and down with Jessica's heavy breathing. Sarah reached for the top button of her blouse and methodically unbuttoned each button. Never releasing her from the intense kiss, Sarah pushed the shirt over Jessica's shoulders. It remained tangled in her pinned arms while Sarah reached behind Jessica and unclasped her bra. Sarah released her grip and moved her hands caressingly down to her hips. Jessica dropped her arms and allowed the blouse and bra to fall to the floor. Sarah's gaze dropped to Jessica's breasts. They were perfect—high and firm and rose tipped, the hard nipples blushed dark.

Jessica backed away briefly and pulled Sarah's tight, white T-shirt over her head. She brushed Sarah's hair from her face, pulled her back to her, and resumed kissing her beautiful lips. Sarah's bare torso pressed against hers, their warm breasts pushing firmly together. Sarah's body was hard and toned from all the physical labor she did. She held Jessica with strong arms wrapped tightly around her.

Jessica moved her hands from Sarah's muscular shoulders down her body over her soft silky skin. She was strong with defined muscles, but she was so soft and sexy, a beautiful woman. Jessica reached for the waistband of Sarah's loose fitting jeans. Sarah inhaled and moaned deep in her throat. This pleasing sound fueled Jessica's impatient hands. She fumbled with the button. Sarah reached down between them to help, but Jessica pushed her hands away and finished the task then moved quickly to unbutton her own jeans. They both backed away slightly and removed their own pants.

Sarah hungrily moved back to Jessica and kissed her behind her ear. Savoring her taste and smell, she lingered on Jessica's sexy long neck. As she pulled her body closer with one hand in the small of her back, Sarah moved her free hand between them and moved aptly through Jessica's neatly trimmed bush. She felt Jessica push into her hand as her fingers moved lightly over her swollen clit. With each attempt Jessica made to move in harder, Sarah lightened her touch teasing her.

"Sarah, please. You're making me crazy." Jessica breathed heavily. Sarah could tell her teasing was having the exact effect she intended.

"I'm about to cum. I can't control this. I need you inside me," Jessica begged.

"Hmm, I like this too much."

Jessica tried again to move over Sarah's hand to push her inside. Sarah met her perfectly and slid her fingers inside her silky wet vagina. Jessica jerked with pleasure. "Yes. Oh yes."

"Cum for me, beautiful." Sarah breathed heavily, equally aroused by the pleasure she was giving.

Sarah felt Jessica's knees give way as she let go and Jessica's legs clamped down on Sarah's hand. "Oh my God! How can you do that?" Jessica leaned heavily on Sarah. "You barely touched me." She tried to catch her breath.

Sarah lowered her to the bed and held her tight next to her. She was totally turned on by Jessica's orgasm. She felt her own wetness around her swollen clit.

Jessica quickly gained her composure and rolled on top of Sarah. "You are absolutely amazing." She began kissing Sarah's breasts—first the right until Sarah's nipple hardened under the touch of her tongue, and then the left. Sarah breathed heavily and moved her legs apart to open herself to Jessica's every touch.

For the second time in as many encounters, they made love all night. Neither able to keep their hands off the other until they nearly passed out from sheer exhaustion.

CHAPTER NINE

Jessica grabbed her phone and hit the answer button to silence the incessant buzzing, but she didn't speak. She held the phone to her ear and fell back onto the fluffy feather pillow and the dream she was living.

"Ms. Whitney, it's Jimmy. Are you there?" The deep sound of Jimmy's voice brought her back to reality.

"Jimmy, yeah I'm here. I'll see you in an hour." She clicked off with no other words. As much as she wanted to come up with some excuses to lie in bed with Sarah all day, she knew she had no choice but to get up and meet Jimmy. She had cut herself to the last minute as it was. When she called him last night, she had been hopeful that she would need every minute of sleep she could get this morning, and she had been right. She felt Sarah move slightly under her, and she realized she was wrapped tightly around Sarah's sexy body. She rolled away, and Sarah turned to nuzzle into her side.

"Hey, beautiful. I've got to get up." She kissed the top of Sarah's head as she tried to slip out of the bed hoping to let Sarah sleep, but Sarah held her down, and she stopped moving. She had quickly realized sometime during the night that if Sarah didn't want her to move, she was not going to move.

"Wait. Just one minute. I just want to feel you next to me for a moment longer," Sarah said as she loosened her tight grip. "I'll make some coffee in just a second."

Jessica obliged and rolled back into Sarah's arms. "You feel amazing. Have I told you how great you make me feel?"

Sarah nuzzled her hair. "I think perhaps you showed me a few times last night." She rose slowly to get out of bed.

"Oh sure, convince me to stay in bed with you and then push me out." Jessica moved to the other side of the bed to get up. Every part of her body was sore, but the memories of how it got that way made every ache worth it.

"I know, I know. What I want and what we both need to do today don't seem to match." Sarah quickly brushed her teeth. She picked up her clothes, still laying exactly where they were dropped on the floor last night, and began pulling them on.

Jessica sat completely naked on the side of the bed, transfixed by Sarah's movements. Jessica knew she could love Sarah. She was afraid she already did. Sarah was everything she had ever dreamed of—intelligent, artistic, mature, and together. Jessica had been with more than a few flaky women. Sarah was so far from that. She was sexy and loving and so damn easy to be with.

"Go get in the shower. It will feel good and wake you up a bit. I'll get the coffee on." Sarah leaned to kiss her, and then she tugged Jessica up off the bed and pointed her in the direction of the bathroom. "I think there is everything you could need in there, but holler if you need anything. There's a clean towel on the hook next to the shower." Jessica followed her instructions.

❖

Benny had taken up her watch detail at the door last night like always and was looking in at the bedroom door when Sarah came out. Seeing Benny standing there brought that familiar and hated pain. "Benny, dammit. You've got to move on. Shit. *We* both have to move on. In my shower is a wonderful woman whom I want to love. Please, please let me." Benny tilted her head, pausing to stare at her before she headed for the back door, toenails clicking across the tile floor.

Sarah followed behind Benny, opened the door, and fell quickly into her morning routine. She had another perfect night with Jessica, and now she felt so conflicted. She wanted to be with her but she felt like she was being unfaithful to Cheryl. Her shoulder muscles tightened, and she had to continually remind herself not to clench her jaw. She cursed herself for feeling that way, but couldn't push the contradictions away. The best she could do was not take it out on Jessica like she did last time.

This was her problem to deal with. It wasn't Jessica's fault. The coffee pot did its thing. She stood in front of it watching the steady flow of dark liquid fill the pot. She tried to focus on the great night forcing out old memories and the guilt. *Dammit, Sarah! Just for a few more minutes until she is gone, and then you can beat yourself up all day long if you want.* Sarah pulled out three mugs. One was a large travel mug. She poured it full and put the lid on it. Her timing was spot-on. As she opened the front door with the coffee in her hand, a black Lincoln sedan pulled up in front of her house.

She barely made it out the door before Jimmy had opened his door and was standing beside the car. "Good morning, Ms. Jarrett," Jimmy said.

"Where's the limo?" She squinted and shaded her eyes from the bright orange sunrise.

"It's in Chicago, ma'am. Ms. Whitney just rents when we're on the road."

"Yes, of course. I brought you some coffee, and you must accept it, or I'll be totally insulted since you wouldn't eat my dinner last night."

"Oh…well…I…ah, thank you, ma'am." Jimmy finally took the cup.

"Do you put anything in it?"

"No, ma'am. I wouldn't ruin a good cup of coffee by putting something in it." He smiled.

"Smart man. She'll be ready in just a few minutes. Would you like to come in?" Sarah moved toward the door.

"No, Ms. Jarrett. I'm much more comfortable out here with the car. Thank you."

Sarah turned back. "Jimmy?"

"Yes, ma'am?"

"Will you do me a favor?"

"Anything, ma'am." He leaned forward giving her his full attention as he awaited her request.

"Please call me Sarah."

"Ahhh, yes, ma'am."

"And no more ma'ams."

"Yes, Ms. Sarah." He smiled at her.

She had to accept that. It was probably as good as it was going to get. When she returned to the house, Jessica was coming out of the bedroom looking beautiful and much more rested and together than Sarah felt.

They met in the front hall and embraced. "Coffee?" Sarah asked as she held her tight and breathed in Jessica's clean smell and felt her hair still slightly damp on her face.

"Thank you, Sarah, but I have to go. I have to get back to the hotel and change and then get to the meeting. I'm hoping I can find a minute to review the drawings so I don't sound like an idiot in the meeting this morning." Jessica was showing the slightest bit of stress.

"I'm sorry. It's my fault you're not prepared." Sarah backed away to let her go.

"You're damn right it is, and I wouldn't trade it for anything, certainly not for an extra minute to prepare for a bunch of prima donnas who have no idea what I'm saying anyway." She relaxed and winked at Sarah and pulled her close again placing her slightly parted lips on Sarah's mouth. Even exhausted, Sarah felt a jolt run through her body as her tongue tangled with Jessica's.

❖

Sarah sat at her kitchen table with her second cup of coffee and toast getting cold in front of her. She was staring at the wall and finally willed herself to move when she heard the thud of Benny's nose nudging the back door to come in. She had to motivate herself to get started on her next project. The cottonwood tree outside would not be producing the money for the bills next month. And she was about to drive to Joe's lumberyard with an embarrassingly small amount of money and ask him again for more credit. She hoped he could help her out one more time, but she hated to ask for yet another favor. He was often strapped himself to keep such a large inventory. They had discussed it often while his workmen loaded her truck.

Finally, she started moving and drove her truck through the city for more lumber. She had the windows rolled down with the wind blowing in her face. She heard the repetitive clicking sound of the tires pulling at the hot asphalt. She pushed the Bluetooth button on her steering wheel and called Patricia.

Patricia picked up on the first ring. "Hey, girl. You have to tell me all about it. Are you just now getting out of bed?"

"No, I didn't just get out of bed," Sarah snapped. "I can't say that I slept much though." Her fingers tightened around the steering wheel as she gave Patricia a little bit of the juicy information she was digging for.

"Way to go, girl."

"She's here in Phoenix for a month."

"Really? That's great. I'm happy for you."

"Why am I feeling so terrible when I spent an amazing night with a gorgeous woman?"

"Sarah, stop it. Please! Please feel good," Patricia said. "You like her, right?"

"Yes, I like her a lot. That's the problem. Don't you get it? It hurts to have feelings for her, but I do."

"Oh, honey. You need to just wallow in this, enjoy the hell out of it. I do get how confusing this might be, but you've got to live." Patricia paused. "Hey, come by my office. We'll go eat lunch—my treat."

"Thanks, Patti, but I have to get started on this project. I'm a day behind already, and I got a slow start today."

"I bet you didn't sleep at all. Hmm, I have memories of all-night sex, but it's been way too long. The memories are so faint." She laughed. "Maybe I'll see if I can get lucky tonight myself, you crazy girl."

Sarah laughed, and she felt better. "I know, right? I'm not as young as I used to be. This is kicking my ass. Today could be a killer."

"Hey, old lady, how are you going to hold up for a month?"

"Yeah, she might just kill me, but at least I'll die happy."

"A month—that means she'll be here for Thanksgiving. You *will* bring her to Thanksgiving dinner."

"Are you kidding? And give Christine the opportunity to embarrass me and give Jessica the third degree?"

"Yes, dear. She has to tolerate it just like we all do, and soon enough she'll love her like the rest of us, even when we would like to kick her in the shin." Patricia laughed.

"Okay. I'll ask her, but if she'd rather not, then that's that. Okay?"

"Sure, whatever. We'll see you both for Thanksgiving. Come over about two—earlier if you can drag yourselves out of bed."

"Hey, thanks, my friend. I'd better go. I'm almost at Joe's."

"Okay, sweetie. Be safe. Don't work out in your shop if you're too tired. No deadline is worth one of your fingers. You know it would have a very negative effect on your sex life." Patricia snickered.

Sarah laughed again and clicked off. Somehow Patricia always knew what to say to make her feel better. Now for Joe.

Sarah parked in front of the big red warehouse and waved at the workmen whom she knew well. She got out and walked slowly into Joe's building. She was dreading this discussion.

"Hey, Sarah." Joe was at the counter in the office building, a small trailer that sat just in front of the large warehouse of lumber.

"Hey, Joe." She stopped in front of the counter and pulled out her wallet. "I only have twelve hundred for you today. I'm so sorry. I know I promised twenty-five, but I just couldn't spread the money out as far as I had hoped." She felt a pang of embarrassment as she handed over a wad of cash.

"Oh," was all he said.

"Joe, you know I'll pay you." She looked at him for some compassion.

"I know, Sarah, but I can't extend your credit any further. I cut everyone else off long before ten K, and you're over that even with this payment. I just can't afford it right now. I'm sorry."

Sarah was even more embarrassed now and didn't quite know what to say. "I know. I understand. You've been very generous. I really appreciate it. I'll get you another payment as soon as I get paid for my next project. I can ask for some money up front and pay you another, probably eight hundred dollars until I get it done, but I have to have about eighty board feet of cherry. I can't pay you back if I'm not building, and I can't build without wood."

"Sarah, that's another five hundred bucks." He tapped his pencil on his calculator.

"Okay…ah…you're right. I'm asking too much." She backed away from the counter a bit. "Maybe Stock's would extend me a bit more." She didn't like Stock's and went there only when Joe didn't have what she needed, but she had to get her lumber somewhere. She turned to go.

"So you're running over to my competitor?"

"Joe, I don't want to, but I understand the bind I'm putting you in, and I have to have the lumber or I can't make any payments." She shrugged. "I'll get you another payment probably a week from Friday. I'll get caught up as soon as I can." She edged closer to the exit.

"Sarah. Damn it, get back over here." He crossed the room in three long strides and put his hand on her shoulder. He guided her back to the counter.

"Can you bring me three K a week from Friday?" He looked at her hopefully.

"I don't know. I'm only getting that much for the project." She paused, doing some math in her head. "I guess I could sell my lathe. I don't use it that much for regular furniture builds, and apparently, my artistic designs are not cutting it." She leaned on the counter, hating the stress she felt from the financial bind the Meyer project had put her in. "Man, I hate to do it, but I guess it's time to smell the coffee."

"I don't want you to compromise your shop."

"No, you're right. I have to get out of debt before I design anymore artistic projects. I have a list of customers, so I have the work. I just have to get to building and stop playing around." Her shoulders dropped as she realized her fate. "Do you know anyone looking for a good lathe?"

"Let's get you that cherry." Joe patted her back. "Jim Nance would probably get you a good price for that lathe. He wouldn't rip you off. I'll give you his number on the way out."

They went out to the warehouse, and Sarah selected the best pieces of cherry and increased her debt by another five hundred and seventy-three dollars, pushing her total debt to Joe to over twelve thousand dollars. Six months of building with no profit was a costly venture, especially since some of the rare exotic woods had cost her in excess of five hundred dollars per board.

❖

Jessica sat silently in the back of the car trying to wrap her brain around the upcoming events of the day, but all she could think about was Sarah.

"Ma'am, are you okay?" Jimmy asked, and she caught his eye in the mirror. She nodded sleepily.

"I was asking, do you want me to wait outside at the hotel or is there something I can do while you change?"

Jessica jerked her head and looked up in the mirror. "I'm sorry. Ah...no just wait. I'll be quick since I've already showered."

"She's very special, ma'am, if you don't mind me saying."

Jessica didn't respond. She was so absorbed in her thoughts she barely heard him. When she finally realized he was waiting for her approval, she spoke up quickly. "Yes, Jimmy. She is, isn't she?" She knew Jimmy was concerned about her. He was usually careful not to comment on anything too personal, but sometimes he couldn't seem to resist giving her a little advice now and then. She realized he wasn't fond of many of the women she had dated in the past. He had no interest in even knowing their names. She was pleased that he liked Sarah, but why wouldn't he? Sarah was real and not interested in her for her name and money. He would be the first to recognize that and she trusted him. "Thanks, Jimmy." She smiled at him as she thought about her evening. She had to get all these emotions under control; she had a business to run.

Jessica made it to her meeting in plenty of time. With Jimmy's shortcuts, she had nearly ten minutes to spare. She was able to settle down and focus so she could get her thoughts together. After the introductions, she quickly began her presentation and was soon in her element. Standing in the front of the boardroom in her business suit and high heels, she owned the room.

Jessica flipped through a dozen slides showing off the new drawings incorporating the requested changes, but maintaining the integrity of her artistic design. Four men in expensive suits and two uptight-looking women from Flag Financing Corporation watched closely as she explained the technical details of the building structure. The room was quiet, and for the first part of the presentation she hardly even got a nod in the form of feedback. After the first few slides, she was finally reassured when they began complimenting her design. Because the construction company was new to her, she stressed her desire to remain in Phoenix through the initial changes. She wasn't convinced the builders understood her wishes, so she was going to make sure they didn't do their own thing. The group expressed their gratitude for her willingness to invest so much in the project, and they would be waiting for her company to send the contract over for signatures later in the week.

Jessica relaxed her tensed shoulders and sat at the conference table. "Thank you all for the opportunity to show you my designs. I'm pleased you like them. We look forward to working with you." She exhaled and began packing her computer into her briefcase. She had taken the first big step in bringing Whitney, Stewart, and Markus out west.

Jessica couldn't deny that she had a secondary motivation for staying in Phoenix, but she was torn by her feelings for Sarah. She made a point of never getting too involved with anyone, her career has always come first. Now here she was getting in deeper and deeper. She didn't want to lose focus on her work; it was all she ever needed before. She definitely wanted to stay as long as she could. Being with Sarah made her contemplate a future with her. Even if her partners wanted her back in Chicago, there really wasn't much she couldn't do from Phoenix. The video teleconference system she arranged would be installed in her hotel room before the end of the day, so she would even be virtually present for most meetings.

At lunch, Jessica made a quick call to Mattie. "Hey, Mattie, it's your favorite boss."

"Oh, Mr. Stewart, your voice sounds very high today," Mattie joked.

"Your loyalty quickly switches when I'm away."

"Ms. Whitney, why are you bugging me? You know I'm jealous of you being all warm in Phoenix while I'm freezing off parts of my body."

"Mattie, can you do something for me? Personal?"

"Why do you even ask? Don't I always? What do you need?"

"Can you get me two tickets to a show here in town? Anything good and the best seats of course."

"Impressing your Phoenix friend, are we?"

"No. I just don't want to be bored in the hotel tonight." Jessica attempted to fib to her.

"And you always need two tickets just in case you want to invite some stranger you see walking down the street." She laughed and then got serious. "I'm glad she called you. Give me an hour. I'll call you back with the information."

"Thank you so much. You're the best. Bye, Mattie." Jessica ate a quick snack and had Jimmy take her over to the offices of the construction company.

She sat down with the CEO and his staff, and they began to contradict her almost immediately. Today, her only purpose was to introduce herself as the new architect and impress them with her work. She would let them know later this week who was in charge of this show. She had been in this business long enough to know, as a woman, she had to change some mindsets before she could get any real work done. She hated it, and often ranted among her coworkers, but she always kept her composure in front of the men she had to appease. Their egos were so fragile. A few minutes into the meeting, her phone rang. Mattie was calling back already.

"Excuse me, gentlemen. I have to take this call." She left the room and answered the phone. "Tell me you found something."

"Well, it's not great, but I got you some tickets to a show."

"What do you mean, not great?"

"I'm not sure theater is their thing out there," Mattie answered, putting on a fake accent.

"Mattie, you city girl, I think you sound more like a Southern bell than a cowgirl. What did you find?"

"It appears from what I could find in short notice, that there are only two theaters of any real significance in Phoenix. The larger one doesn't have a show tonight and the smaller one is showing…guess what?"

"Mattie, seriously, I just walked out of a meeting with a bunch of contractors to take your call. I can't be rude forever." She sounded a bit short, but truthfully, she didn't care how long she kept the arrogant Neanderthals waiting. They would do what she said one way or another, or she would make sure they didn't build her project or anything else in Phoenix ever again. However, she liked to make them think they were compromising. She smiled at herself.

"Sorry, Ms. Whitney." Mattie got serious. "The Arizona Broadway Theatre is playing *Chicago*, believe it or not. I know you've seen it a few dozen times, but it was the only thing I could find. Also, no box seats, but I was able to pull some strings and get front row seats. I already talked to Jimmy. He's going to pick them up as soon as I call him back with your approval."

"That sounds great. You're my hero. What time is the show, and what do they wear here? Seems to be much less formal than, well, anywhere I've ever been."

"The show starts at eight, but I'm afraid you're on your own with the Western attire. Cowboy boots?" Mattie laughed out loud. "Oh Ms. Whitney, that is a funny visual."

"Hmm, I'll have to work this out. Thank you for the tickets. You're wonderful. I'll see you in a few weeks."

Jessica returned to the meeting. She could see the men were impatient with her. It might be time to give them a little something. She schmoozed with them and complimented their work for the next hour or so until she couldn't take it anymore. "Gentlemen, let's discuss this further tomorrow. I'll be here at nine in the morning." Without giving them a chance to respond, she walked out of the room.

As she left the conference room, she saw a small, older woman at the reception area. "Can you help me?"

"Yes, ma'am. What do you need?"

"I'm going to a play at the Arizona Broadway Theatre, and I'm not from here. I was wondering what the appropriate attire is for something like that out here."

"You mean out West, ma'am?" She smiled and gave her a kind, knowing look. "I'm afraid you will see everything in that theater tonight from flip-flops to formal gowns. Somewhere between here and the Mississippi, that type of style etiquette got lost. You will surely not be out of place no matter what you wear, but I can't imagine you have flip-flops."

"I see. So slacks and a sweater would be fine?"

"Perfect."

"Okay good. You're very kind." Jessica smiled at her.

"We might not know how to dress for a show, but we know how to be hospitable. Enjoy the show."

"Thank you so much." Jessica waved and walked to the elevator. It was after three. She had forgotten to call Sarah. *Oh great, Jess. Arrange a date and forget to ask the girl. You may have two tickets for nothing, you idiot.*

She pulled up Sarah's number on her phone and connected.

"Hey. How's the smart, talented architect doing? Kicking ass and takin' names I assume?"

"I'm very good. I'm not sure about any ass kicking though. How's the hot woodworker?"

"I bet you'd like to know if I'm covered in sawdust, wouldn't you?"

"Well, since you asked..." Jessica did have a quick flash of Sarah wearing a tool belt. "Stop that," she said. "I mean, I was wondering if you would go to the theater with me tonight." Jessica struggled to get the words out. She always got so nervous when she was asking someone out.

"You're asking me on a date?"

"Yes. I'm asking you on a date. I have two tickets to see *Chicago* at the Arizona Broadway Theatre. I'd like you to join me. Don't give me a hard time."

"I'm not sure our shows will compare with what you get in the Second City."

"Have you been to this theater before?" Jessica was worried that it wasn't a nice place. Mattie would never do something like that to her. Knowing Mattie, she called everyone she could think of until she found references.

"I have. It's small, but a classy venue." She paused. "I would love to go with you to the show."

"Great! It starts at eight. Jimmy and I will be by to pick you up at about seven. Is that okay?" Jessica was excited to take Sarah someplace nice. She finally got on the elevator and rode it to the ground floor.

Jimmy was waiting for her at a little coffee bar with a book in one hand. She sometimes thought he was psychic, because he was standing up walking toward her as the elevator door opened. "Ms. Whitney, you're supposed to call me so I can have the car ready."

"Oh, Jimmy. I think I can walk to the car. Besides, the fresh air and warm sun will feel good. Were you able to pick up the show tickets?"

"Yes, ma'am. I have them here." He put his hand over the breast pocket of his black suit jacket.

"Thank you."

They reached the car and Jimmy opened the door for her. She crawled in and was asleep before he pulled out of the parking lot.

"Ma'am." He spoke softly to wake her. "We're at the hotel."

"Thanks, Jimmy. Wow I was out." She raised her head. "We'll need to leave to pick up Ms. Jarrett in time to be at the show before the curtain at eight. Please call me about an hour before you would like to depart."

"Yes, ma'am. I'm going to get the car washed, and I'll be back. Ma'am, you'll need this." He handed her the phone. She was always leaving it in the car.

Jessica smiled at him and took the phone. She had a love/hate relationship with that phone. Jessica walked through the front doors and strolled through the lobby. With her key card inserted, she pushed the button for the Presidential Suite—her home for the next four weeks.

That quick nap had revived her, and now her task was to put together the perfect outfit for tonight. She wanted something simple. She spotted her black slacks. She found an off-white cashmere sweater. *That works.* From her jewelry box she pulled out a string of pearls and matching earrings—*classy or classic?* She wanted to look hot, not old. She decided it was elegant and would work fine. When she went back to the closet for shoes and saw her black cocktail dress. *No…this. It's short and sexy—much better than classy or classic.*

Jessica showered quickly and put her hair up, and instead of pearls, she went for a more subtle diamond pendant surrounded by small ruby stones. As she stood in front of the mirror, she was worried that she had gone over the top. *Oh well, here goes nothing.* She pulled out a lightweight black wool cap. She sat at her computer to make sure there were no crises from work that couldn't wait for tomorrow and was relieved to see everything was fine. Jessica grabbed her small black Gucci bag and got in the elevator.

The hotel concierge boldly addressed her. "Ma'am, you look amazing." Jimmy gave him an evil eye, and he shrank back behind his desk.

"Thank you so much." Jessica smiled at the young man.

Jimmy extended his arm, and she wrapped her arm around his elbow. "Ms. Whitney, you look lovely.There are a few folks in this room whose tongues nearly hit the floor."

"Too much, you think?" she asked, nervously twisting the straps of her purse.

"No, ma'am. Just enough I'd say."

They drove the short distance to Sarah's with only a few words exchanged. When they pulled up, Jimmy started to get out and go to the door.

"Jimmy, are you going to get my date?" she teased him as she opened her own door.

"Oh no. Sorry, ma'am. I'll be right here." He got back in the car.

Jessica walked to the door and heard Benny bark even before she rang the bell.

Sarah opened the door and stared for a minute. "You look amazing." She looked down at her gray pinstripe slacks and red silk blouse. "I'm way underdressed."

"No, you look great. We match perfectly. That's a beautiful diamond pendant." Jessica lightly touched Sarah's neck where the small elegant necklace hung.

"Thank you," Sarah said as she looked up at Jessica. "You're so tall! How will I kiss you?" Jessica leaned down and kissed Sarah. "That'll work." Sarah smiled at her.

"Shall we go?" Jessica took her hand.

Sarah gave Benny a pat on the head and locked the door as they left. She followed Jessica to the car where Jimmy stood holding the door.

"Good evening, Jimmy."

"Good evening, Ms. Sarah."

They rode quietly in the car holding hands in the back until Sarah finally blurted out, "Jess, how do you feel about Thanksgiving?"

"Well, I think it's a great idea. Let's set aside a day each year on a Thursday. Let's say, the last week of November, and we'll all have a really big meal at harvest time and be thankful. I'm in."

Sarah ignored her. "My best friends, Patricia and Christine, uh, well, I always have Thanksgiving with them, and they desperately want to meet you."

"Yes, yes, I want to meet your friends."

"Oh, damn. Sorry. I mean that's too bad. I was hoping you would say no."

"Really? You don't want me to go?" Jessica was confused.

"No, that's not it. It's just…Christine is going to say something or several somethings to embarrass me, and she will be relentless with questions for you. It could be quite painful."

"I can handle it. I deal with some of the stiffest, crankiest, skeptical, old men you'd ever meet nearly every day. I can handle this."

"Oh my poor, innocent, big city girl. You don't know my lawyer friend, but okay, we'll go. And despite the pain, I want you to meet them. They are two of the best people I know. They have always been there for me. I owe them so much."

They pulled up in front of the theater. Jimmy ran around the car and opened the door. The people standing outside were staring at the big shiny Lincoln. Sarah got out first and held out her hand for Jessica.

"Ma'am, here are the tickets." Jimmy held out a small white envelope for Jessica.

Jessica took it, and she and Sarah walked in holding hands.

They had arrived just in time. Most of the other seats were already filled. Sarah would've never cut it so close. Her old military mind caused her to always be early—often way too early. The usher took them all the way to the front of the auditorium. Sarah felt all the eyes in the room watching the gorgeous woman walking in front of her. Almost as soon as they sat down, the house light dimmed, and Jessica took Sarah's hand. Sarah leaned over to whisper in her ear. "If I forget to tell you later, I had a great time. Thank you."

"You are a hopeless romantic. You're Julia Roberts in *Pretty Woman*." Jessica laughed.

"I wondered if you would get that reference, but I actually feel more like Richard Gere with the pretty woman. Did you happen to notice that the whole room watched you walk in?"

"Don't be silly. They were looking at you." Jessica squeezed her hand and then the music began as if on cue.

The show was fun, a small scale but talented rendition of a snazzy musical full of gorgeous dancers and passionate singers. Sarah was relieved. She had been concerned that she would be embarrassed for her Western city. At intermission, they went out to get some fresh air. The theater was small and stuffy, and the chill in the air outside felt refreshing.

"Jessica Whitney?" A tall, burly man in a wrinkled, too-small suit lumbered over to them. "I see you do stop working occasionally." Sarah tried to release Jessica's hand, but Jessica held tight. Sarah felt a rush of adrenaline as the big man approached. While Sarah would never go back in the closet with her sexual orientation, she didn't feel the need to put herself or her date at risk. She had seen and heard of too many situations where some small-minded people did something stupid because they weren't ready to accept the changing world they lived in.

Jessica finally released Sarah's hand to receive the man's outstretched hand. "Good evening, Rod. I didn't take you for a theater guy." She looked over at Sarah. "Rodney Wilson, this is Sarah Jarrett. She's a local artist and craftsman. Sarah, this is Rodney Wilson. His dad owns the contracting company that's going to construct my building. He doesn't like my design." Sarah couldn't help but hear the emphasis Jessica put on the "my" when referring to her building.

"I'm the vice president of Wilson Contracting," he said. "And that's not true. I love your design. I just think we're going to have to make a few changes to ensure solid construction and to meet all code requirements."

"It sure is a good thing I spent so many years in college learning good construction techniques, and the past year researching and understanding Arizona building codes has come in handy while creating this design." Her frustration with this man was clear in her sarcasm. "But, Rod, we should discuss this tomorrow. We came here to enjoy the show. You have an amazing theater company here."

"Very good point. So, Ms. Jarrett, what type of art do you create?"

"Ms. Whitney exaggerates a bit. I build custom wood furniture," Sarah said. She looked across the street. She didn't want to make eye contact with this man Jessica clearly didn't like.

"I do not exaggerate. I'm thinking of asking the buyer to commission her work for the top floor offices."

"What? I'm not sure that—" Sarah started.

"I'm planning to set up a meeting later this month. We'll talk then," Jessica continued.

"Interesting," Rod Wilson said. "Well, I'll let you two figure that out. There is one thing I would like to ask you about, Jessica."

"Excuse me, please." Sarah found a way to escape. "I see they have a wine bar. Would either of you like a glass of wine?"

"Yes, please. I'll come with you. Tomorrow, Rod. I'll answer all your questions tomorrow." Jessica grabbed Sarah's hand, and they both escaped.

Jessica bent to Sarah's ear. "You were going to leave me out there with that ignorant Philistine."

Sarah moved quickly ahead of her. They were attached, but Sarah wanted to get away. She stopped and turned to Jessica. "What do you mean contract me for designs?" Her voice was slightly elevated. The people nearest them in the lobby turned to see who was talking.

"Sarah," Jessica said in a harsh voice. "Your work would be amazing for the design. The experience you have with Southwestern design and style is exactly what we need. Why wouldn't you do it?"

"How's that going to look? You get a gig for the woman you're sleeping with?"

"Calm down, please. I don't mind if people know I sleep with women, especially the beautiful, angry woman in front of me, but I'd rather not discuss this so loudly in front of everyone." She spoke quietly as she moved them to the corner of the room. The lights flickered to indicate intermission was over. "You're right. I should have talked to you before I brought it up like that, but this has nothing to do with who I sleep with. I don't work like that. Your work is amazing. Can we talk about this later and just enjoy our evening?" Jessica leaned over to kiss her, and Sarah tried to turn away. "Sarah, kiss me!" Jessica insisted. Her beautiful, red lips were hard to resist. Sarah returned the kiss and that rush of arousal pumped through her as it did every time Jessica touched her like that. "Okay?"

"Okay." They walked hand in hand back to their seats, having missed the opportunity to get a drink.

When the show ended, Jessica pulled Sarah to one of the emergency exits on the side of the auditorium. "Where are we going?"

"Follow me." She giggled like a little girl. When she opened the door, the Lincoln was parked in the alley, and Jimmy stood with the door open. They climbed in.

"Seriously—are you psychic, Jimmy?" Sarah asked.

"No, Ms. Sarah. I've just been doing this for a long time. I find all the tricks." He was pleased with himself. "It only works when Ms. Whitney remembers to bring her phone, and I can text her." He shot a glare through the reflection in the mirror. "She has a tendency to leave it in the backseat."

"What did you say?" Jessica teased him.

"Nothing, ma'am."

Jessica wrapped her arms around Sarah's neck and then threw one sexy long leg over Sarah's lap. "That was a very good show. Thank you for coming with me."

All anger had vanished. Sarah pulled Jessica into a kiss, pushing her tongue through open, waiting lips. Jessica tangled her tongue with Sarah's, and the petting heated up quickly. Sarah remembered where she was and that they were not alone. She pulled away and felt her face flush red. Sarah clinched her jaw and looked toward Jimmy. Jessica followed her gaze. "He doesn't mind."

"I do."

"Then come up to my room with me tonight," she said, kissing and lightly licking Sarah's neck and ear.

"I don't think I could resist if I wanted to."

"Jimmy, we're going to the hotel," Jessica said. He simply nodded knowingly.

"I was hoping you would say that. Jimmy can take you home in the morning or you could stay and enjoy room service all day tomorrow."

"Well, as appealing as that sounds, I think I'll have to pass on the all-day room service, but you might need it since I don't plan to let you sleep again tonight."

"Promises, promises." They were tangled in a deep kiss again as they pulled up to the Ritz-Carlton.

"Wow. You never do anything halfway, do you?" Sarah said as she realized they had just drove up to the best hotel in Phoenix. Jessica pulled her out of the car. "Wait, what time are you taking me home tomorrow?" Sarah looked back in the car as Jimmy got out.

He looked over the top of the car. "What time would you like me to take you, Ms. Sarah?" He looked at Jessica as he asked the question, and Sarah did too.

"I have a nine o'clock, so if you leave here at eight you should be back in time to get me to the meeting." She turned to

Sarah. "Or you can wait until I get back, and Jimmy can take you at nine thirty."

"Eight is perfect. I can get home and let Benny out. See you then, Jimmy, and thank you."

"My pleasure, ma'am...I mean, Ms. Sarah."

Sarah followed Jessica through the mostly empty lobby to the elevator in the back of the hall. Jessica used her card and pushed the button to the Presidential Suite.

"The Presidential Suite?"

"It's the best, says Richard Gere to the Pretty Woman." Jessica thrust Sarah against the elevator and pushed her dress up exposing tops of her silk stockings and a lacy garter belt.

"Oh my God! Are you trying to kill me? You're so fucking hot...sorry, I mean you're so hot!" Sarah pulled her close and kissed her deeply, breathing heavily with desire. She stopped and pushed her away. Jessica backed away, her face pained. "They have cameras in these elevators. Don't you watch TV?"

The door opened to a large full suite living space. Sarah couldn't remember ever being in a room quite like this. "Wow." She stopped in her tracks not quite knowing what to do.

"This way. There are no cameras in here." Jessica pulled her to the large bedroom and pushed her onto the king-sized bed. They made love with the passion of the first time.

"You feel amazing lying on top of me," Sarah spoke to the top of Jessica's head as she smoothed her silky dark hair away from her face. Jessica started to roll off of her, but Sarah held her still. "Stay here. Fall asleep here."

"Mmm, be careful what you wish for. I could be asleep in a minute."

"Good. Relax." Jessica lay perfectly still for a few minutes and then pulled Sarah over with her so they were facing each other. "I've never met anyone like you." Jessica stroked Sarah's face, moving strands of hair aside.

"Hmm, is that a good thing?"

"It's a great thing. I can't seem to get enough of you. Every time you fulfill me, you also create a new desire." Jessica kissed Sarah's face.

"What are you doing tomorrow night?" Sarah asked, changing the soft mood.

"Umm. Well I was hoping..." Jessica ran her hand down Sarah's thigh.

"I'm taking you out tomorrow. Do you have some Levi's?"

"Jeans? I have jeans. I don't think I have Levi's. Do they have to be a particular brand? Am I going to be committing a fashion faux pas?"

"It's not so much a fashion issue as a comfort issue." Sarah contemplated a minute. "I bet you would fit in mine if your legs weren't so damn long...and sexy." Sarah moved her hand between Jessica's inner thighs.

"If you want me to wear jeans, I can do that. I'm quite comfortable in my jeans, but if it's that important I can ask Jimmy to pick up some Levi's tomorrow."

"You kill me." Sarah laughed at her. "You get everything you want, don't you?"

"Yes!" She kissed her intimately. "But right now all I want is you."

"You got me." Sarah returned the kiss. "Don't go buying new jeans, you crazy woman. Just wear something comfortable and easy to move around in. And very casual. What about tennis shoes—do you have tennis shoes?"

"Of course. I'm a runner." Jessica seemed a little put out. "What must you think of me?"

"What do you mean? I didn't mean anything. It's just you have very nice clothes. You have very nice everything. I want to take you somewhere, well, nice clothes just aren't appropriate."

Jessica relaxed again. "Where are you taking me? Are we going to be rolling in mud or something?"

"As exciting as that sounds, there will be no rolling in mud. It's a surprise." Sarah teased her. "I'll be here at six tomorrow. We'll eat first."

"Jimmy can—"

"No Jimmy. Give the poor man a night off. Do you mind riding in a truck?"

"Seriously, do you think that I think I'm too good to ride in a truck?" The flare of anger sparked again.

"I'm sorry. I'm being a little small, aren't I?" She raised Jessica's chin and kissed her lips.

"Tomorrow, six, jeans, truck. I'm excited." Jessica's big smile made her look like a teenage girl preparing for her first date.

"Great! Now let's try and see if I can fulfill your desires." Sarah rolled her on her back and slid down to the ample swells of her breasts, placing her mouth over them one at a time until she felt Jessica's nipple harden beneath her tongue. Jessica groaned and rose to meet her mouth. Sometime later, they finally fell asleep with the blankets twisted around them.

❖

The sound of the phone brought them back to reality again way too soon.

Jessica answered and put the phone back in the cradle then turned and reached out for Sarah. She was already out of the bed pulling on her clothes from last night. She had managed to lay them across the chair so they weren't quite as wrinkled as she feared. She borrowed Jessica's toothbrush and washed her face quickly.

"Hey, beautiful. You better get up. I'm heading downstairs. Jimmy will be back in an hour." She leaned down and kissed her. "I'll see you tonight." She smiled at her. "Are you awake?"

Jessica smiled back. "I'm awake. You tasted good. Come back here, and I'll show you how awake I am."

"Thanks for the toothbrush." Sarah rushed to the door. "Neither of us will get to work if I come back to that bed."

"Chicken," Jessica yelled as Sarah got in the elevator.

"You got that right." The doors closed on her.

Jimmy was waiting in the lobby. "Good morning, Ms. Sarah."

"Hi, Jimmy. Do you mind that you have to drag her short-term lover around all month?"

"Short-term?" Jimmy stopped and looked Sarah directly in the eye. "I hope you don't think this is a regular thing with her." He was direct. "She likes you. I know it's none of my business, but you should know she is really a good person—one of the best. I've been with her for a long time, and I've never seen her like this. She has had some dates now and then, but mostly all she does is work. Do I mind taking you wherever you need to go?" He looked at her with a stern, serious, and scary expression. "Ms. Sarah, I'm pleased to do it. You make her happy."

"I'm sorry, Jimmy. I didn't—"

"It's okay. I'm the one who shouldn't be butting in."

They walked in silence to the car. Sarah, while feeling slightly embarrassed by the scolding she had just received, was pleased to hear Jimmy's thoughts, yet scared of them as well. The label of short-term was to protect herself, and he was forcing her to realize how false it was.

Sarah finally broke the silence. She didn't want it to be weird between her and Jimmy. "I'm taking Jessica on a date tonight. I would like to pick her up at the door, but it just occurred to me I can't really do that. Do you have a suggestion?"

"What time are you picking her up?" he asked without looking up at the mirror.

"Six."

"I'll be in the lobby. I have a key card. I'll let you in her elevator." Jimmy frowned at her in the mirror.

"Thank you, Jimmy." He finally smiled when he looked back.

CHAPTER TEN

Jessica arrived at Wilson Contracting's conference room at exactly nine o'clock.

"Rough night, Ms. Whitney?" Rodney sneered.

"No. You?" She stared him down. "Yesterday, we were talking about some construction issues. Let's pick up where we left off." She allowed no time for small talk. "I have some images I put together of similarly constructed buildings, and I can go over them in detail—each part of the reinforcement and construction if you would like. I also understand someone has concerns about code compliance." She looked directly at Rodney. "I've scheduled a late conference call with two draftsmen who worked on all the code issues. They'll address your fears, Rodney."

She pressed through the presentation with no time for questions. After going for almost two hours straight, George Wilson stopped her. "Ms. Whitney, you've convinced me. I need a break. When we return, we'll see if there are other matters that need to be addressed."

Jessica started putting papers away. She would go back to the buyer with the results and perhaps even get back to the hotel early this afternoon to sit in on the office staff meeting via VTC.

"We're not done here." Rodney approached her.

"I don't recall any other concerns from yesterday." Jessica didn't look up from her papers.

"Well, I have more. I want to discuss some more issues with your design. You're failing to abide by a number of codes." He paused. "Was that your girlfriend last night?"

"Rodney, that's none of your business. I have other work today. I've answered the initial questions. If you are available for the conference call with my draftsmen this afternoon, they'll answer any questions you have about Arizona building codes." She looked him directly in the eye. "Construction can begin on time. Send any questions you have to my office. I have a staff that will follow up with any other issues." She knew there was nothing wrong with the drawing, especially no code violations.

"You're pretty sure of yourself, aren't you?"

"Yes." She finally looked up at him.

The room filled up again, and George Wilson stood up. "Is there anything else any of you would like Ms. Whitney to discuss?"

No one said a word. Even Rodney sat quietly in the corner.

"Excellent. Great work. We look forward to building a beautiful building with you." He started clapping, and the whole room joined in.

"Mr. Wilson, I'll be available locally for the next three weeks. I'll be on the job site when I can. I won't take any more of your time today." Jessica shook Mr. Wilson's hand and grabbed her briefcase, pushing her laptop inside and left the room.

❖

Sarah had prepared all the wood for the next build. Nearly eighty board feet of cherry had been surfaced, squared, and planed to thickness. She was surprised at how much she got finished in one day. She often overestimated how much work she could do. The wood needed a few days to acclimate before she could start the build. To keep busy while she let it dry, Sarah pulled out some leftover pieces of exotic wood so she could work on some small projects for an art show coming up this spring. Small, creative jewelry boxes sold well at the local art shows, and she had plenty of wood to build them. It was a good way to make a little extra cash during down time between big projects and use up some small pieces of wood. She would start on that tomorrow. She was done with plenty of time to clean the truck. She headed for the door, and Benny jumped up to follow her out of the shop.

Sarah was going to be early. At least she wouldn't be able to embarrass herself by knocking on Jessica's door since she couldn't get in without Jimmy's help. The parking lot was a bit of an obstacle course for a full-sized pickup truck, but she finally found a spot in the back that was big enough for the truck. She still had plenty of time so she stopped to take in the brilliant oranges of the sunset. She'd been going nonstop for the past few weeks and had barely given herself time to think. But thinking wasn't good. She questioned her feelings each time she thought about it. Jimmy's words this morning still echoed in her ears. *"She likes you."*

What does that mean? Will she expect something of me? Should I end it now? She didn't want to end it. Sarah had no idea she could ever feel like this again. It was scary to think that someone else could make her feel the way she felt with Cheryl. She never dreamed anyone else could make her feel alive again. She looked down at her watch—almost six. She started walking to the doors and remembered the flowers in the truck and rushed back to get them, then trotted to the front doors. Jimmy was standing at the entrance waiting for her. He was still in his ever-present, uncompromising black suit.

"Ms. Sarah," he said.

"Thanks, Jimmy." Jimmy escorted her to the elevator and swiped the key.

"Have fun." He handed her a business card. "Call me if you drink too much or…if you need anything."

"Jimmy!" She just shook her head as the doors closed.

In seconds, the doors opened to the suite, and Jessica was sitting on the sofa watching as the doors opened. She smiled when she saw Sarah.

"It's hard to surprise you."

Jessica got up and walked to her, wearing a new pair of Levi's and a long sleeve blue T-shirt and new red converse tennis shoes. She looked like a runway model showing off her Western look.

Sarah met her, and they embraced with a long kiss. "Nice jeans." She held out the arrangement of fall-colored flowers. "These are for you."

"Is this a full-service date?"

"I guess we'll see about that later." Sarah blushed. "I'm a little old-fashioned."

"They're beautiful. Thank you. I prefer to think of you as traditional, not old-fashioned, and I like traditional." She took the flowers and pulled out a vase from the cabinet in the full bar in the corner of her suite. She put water in it and set the flowers on the table in the center of the room.

"Shall we go?" Sarah asked.

"We shall." They boarded the elevator. As they walked across the lobby, Sarah saw Jimmy watching them from the far corner of the room. She wondered if he would worry all night.

"The truck is in the back. It was the only spot I could find. I'll drive around to pick you up."

"You're kidding, right? Is that a rich girl joke?"

"No. It's part of the full-service date." She was trying to be chivalrous.

"I'll follow you to the truck, you crazy woman."

Sarah opened the passenger door and held out her arm for Jessica to boost herself up. "Wow! I didn't realize how big it was."

Sarah laughed. "I know. No one ever really knows how big *it* is. Maybe I'm compensating for small breasts." And they both laughed. Sarah climbed in the other side and pulled out of the parking lot.

"I like the view from up so high." Jessica looked around. "Where are we going?"

"How do you feel about burgers? I wanted the whole night to be a surprise, but the place I'm really craving isn't at all good for you, and if you would hate it then I don't want to take you there."

"A burger actually sounds wonderful. I can't remember the last time I had a really good burger."

"I was hoping you would say that. I'm going to get you the best burger you've ever eaten."

"You should've told me to get a larger size in my Levi's." She patted her flat stomach.

They shared the events of their day on the short drive to Tonto's Bar and Grill.

"I managed to get all the wood prepared for my next project despite my sleep-deprived state."

"That's great. Now I don't have to feel guilty about keeping you up."

"Oh no, you should still feel guilty." Sarah reached across the wide seat for Jessica's hand and squeezed. "How was your day?"

"I was pretty frustrated with Rodney Wilson. He couldn't resist bringing up last night. I think I generally do pretty well at not letting guys like that get under my skin, but he almost succeeded today."

"He sounds like an asshole." Sarah caught herself. "Sorry. That was uncalled for. I mean he doesn't sound like a nice man." Sarah pulled into the large parking lot in the back of the bar.

Jessica laughed at her. "You're always afraid of offending me."

Sarah punched her lightly in the arm and ran around to open her door. Jessica opened her own door and slid out before Sarah could get there.

Sarah nodded to one of the waitresses who was standing next to the bar when they entered. Then she headed for the wooden patio in the back of the building. There were only a few tables on the patio, and only one other couple sitting outside. It was quieter on the patio. The propane heaters set up around the perimeter created a comfortable environment despite the cool evening. Sarah chose a table in the corner farthest from the other couple and the rest of the bar. "Is this okay or do you think you'll be cold out here?"

"No, this is great."

"Okay. So here's the deal. Monica is a friend of mine. Her daughter was in my squadron when I was still on active duty. She deployed with me to Iraq."

"Colonel, it has been way too long."

Sarah stood to give her a hug, and Monica gave her a huge bear hug that practically knocked her down.

"Monica, this is my friend Jessica. Jess, this is Monica."

"Hmm, you got yourself a real pretty one here, Sarah." She smiled at Jessica, took her hand, and pulled her up into a hug. "No handshakes for me. Nice to meet you." Monica squeezed Jessica with the same intensity.

Jessica looked a little stunned, caught her balance and said, "Nice to meet you, too."

"How's Robin? Is she still out East? I haven't heard from her in a while," Sarah asked.

"She's doing great. She tested for Technical Sergeant a month or so ago. And she's going to be moving somewhere in Texas for her next assignment. I'm glad she'll be a little closer. I'll tell her I saw you. Now, what can I get you ladies to drink? Hefeweizen for you, Colonel?"

"You remembered. Do you like beer, Jess? I'm afraid I forgot—they only serve beer here. You have wine too, don't you?"

"I'll have the same." Jessica jumped in quickly, and Monica disappeared to get the drinks

"I'm not too good at this. It's been a long time since I've been on a date."

"Don't be silly. This place is quaint, and I love it."

"Really?"

"Really, and I'm with you, so of course I love it."

Sarah blushed.

"What is this stuff about colonel? You were a colonel...are a colonel? That's a big deal. You didn't tell me you were a big deal."

"First of all, I was a Lieutenant Colonel, and secondly, it never felt like a big deal to me. It was my job—what I loved."

"You should be proud of your service and your accomplishments."

Sarah was blushing again and steered the subject away from herself. "I should warn you the burgers here are huge."

"Let's split it. I'm quite sure I can't eat one by myself."

Monica returned with the beers. "Now what are we eating tonight?"

"Bring us the house burger with cheddar, and would you ask the cook to cut it in half?" Sarah ordered without looking at the menu.

"Done." Monica scribbled on her notepad. "I'll get this in." She touched Sarah's shoulder and winked at her while throwing a glance at Jessica.

Jessica looked at Sarah when Monica walked away. "You sure did make quite an impression on her. You must have been very good at your work in the military. Do you mind telling me about it?"

"There's not much to tell. We were lucky. It was scary there, but the group I deployed with all came home safely. It's one of those things that's difficult to explain. I don't have any bad stories, but it was hard to be there. I'm extremely proud of all the people who deployed with me. We did really good work."

"I'm sorry. I shouldn't have brought it up." Jessica took Sarah's hand.

"No, it's okay. It's not like that. I just don't really know how to explain it. Mostly, it was really long hours and lots of work." Sarah smiled to show it was okay. She didn't want Jessica to worry about her time in Iraq. Monica saved her by returning with their food. While they ate they listened to country and western music from the live band playing in the bar.

❖

"You were right. That was the best burger I've ever had," Jessica said as she climbed back in Sarah's truck. "I'm so glad you recommended splitting it though. It was huge."

Sarah laughed. "You seem to be experiencing a lot of very big things tonight."

"What are you, a twelve-year-old boy?" Jessica was the one doing the arm punching this time.

"No, ma'am. I am not, thank you very much. I'll prove it to you a little later if you want."

"Don't tease." Jessica smiled at her.

"Are you ready for the fun?" Sarah started the truck and turned on her iPad. Tori Amos came softly through the speakers with "A Sorta Fairytale."

"There's more? I had a great time already. The music was very...ah..."

"Country," Sarah finished for her.

"Yes, country. I enjoy your selections much better, but I did like the band. They were good for a local group."

"You don't get out much, do you?" Sarah couldn't keep from smiling. "When was the last time you were in a bar like that? No, the real question is, have you ever been in a bar like that?"

"In college a bunch of us drove down to Virginia one summer and—stop, you're teasing me."

"Well, it's my turn to watch you feel a little out of place." Sarah was watching the road. "Do you realize I've never even been in a suite like your hotel? The bathroom is bigger than my workshop."

"Do you have a point? So we grew up a little differently."

"A little differently. Hmm, okay. Doesn't it concern you at all that I'm barely hanging on to middle class?"

"Should it? I mean do you need some help?"

"No!" she barked harshly. "I wasn't telling you so you would offer me money. I was pointing out how different we are."

"Sarah, please stop. I'm having such a good time. I don't want to talk about something we can't change and doesn't matter anyway," Jessica said in a low voice.

"You're right." They rode quietly for the next mile until a perfectly harmonized duet began singing a love song.

"I like this song. You have good taste in music."

"Thank you. I'm sorry if I was being stupid."

"It's okay."

"Good, because we're here." Sarah pulled off the highway at Bob's Go-Karts.

Jessica looked around and saw the sign and grinned from ear to ear. "I have always wanted to do this."

"Don't tell me you've never driven a go-kart?"

"I haven't ever driven a go-kart, but I'm going to beat you. You'll show me how?" Jessica wrestled with her seat belt as she hurried to get out of the truck. "I'm so excited."

Sarah was thrilled that she had picked something Jessica was excited about and had never done. "I'm not going to teach you if you are already bragging about beating me."

Jessica grabbed Sarah's hand and started swinging their arms back and forth. She pulled Sarah along, skipping up to the door. Jessica's excitement was contagious, and any bad feelings about socio-economic class were left for another day.

"Good evening, ladies." A tall, weathered man with sun-tanned, wrinkled skin greeted them with a husky smoker's rasp as they entered. "You girls interested in a go-kart race?" He stood stooped over, behind a worn plywood counter wearing a dusty old cowboy hat, faded Wranglers, and a flannel shirt.

Before Sarah had a chance to answer, Jessica blurted out, "We want to drive the karts. Give me your fastest one."

"All right. Let's get you fixed up. A standard race is fourteen laps, but if you buy three races, you can save twenty percent. "

"We want three!" Jessica started to pull her wallet out.

"Excuse me. This is my treat." Sarah put her hand over Jessica's wallet and pushed it away.

"Oh, yeah. Sorry." She was bouncing up and down next to Sarah.

"Ma'am, why don't you go over there and pick out a helmet? The cars are just in that corner there." He pointed across the track. "They all run fine. I should know I'm the one that keeps them running, so you pick any one you want."

He totaled the bill and handed it to Sarah. She handed him her credit card. This would be a small addition to her already grossly extended credit, but it would be worth every penny.

Sarah walked to the karts with a helmet in hand. "Oh, I see you picked the yellow one. I wouldn't have pegged you for liking yellow."

"No, I hate yellow, but yellow cars go faster." She was already sitting in the car that was pinned behind two others.

"Hmm, you have science to back that up, do you?"

"Ma'am, if you'll get up for a minute I'll get that one out for you." The man attempted to project his gravelly voice across the row of cars.

Sarah looked around. "We have the track to ourselves?"

As he pushed around the karts to get to the one Jessica selected, he answered her. "You probably have time for all three of your races before the teenagers hit the track. You're a little early for that crowd."

"Perfect." Jessica's smile seemed permanently fixed on her face.

He pushed Jessica's chosen car to the start line and lumbered back over to the parked cars. "Okay, ma'am. Which one do you want?"

Sarah picked a green one in front. "I'll take this one."

He pushed it over beside Jessica, who was already buckled up and playing with the buttons in the car.

"Okay. You ladies know what you're doing?" Sarah nodded and Jessica just continued to smile, looking anxious to push the gas pedal. "I can't imagine you all would cause me too much trouble, but the list of rules are there on the wall. Keep your helmets on and seat belts buckled at all times. Have fun, girls." He winked at Jessica and walked across the track back to the counter.

"I say we have a little wager here," Sarah said, looking at Jessica's beaming face. "You're like a kid."

"I know. I'm just anxious to kick your butt. What's your wager?"

"Okay. Let's just say we make the first race a practice race, and the winner of the second race makes coffee tomorrow morning."

"Is that an invitation to spend the night with you?" Jessica winked at her.

"It's part of the full-service date." Sarah winked back.

"I have a better idea—best two out of three makes coffee." Jessica barely finished before she hit the gas.

"Oh, you sneak!" Sarah yelled and hit her own gas.

They raced around the figure-eight track. Sarah watched as Jessica slowed at each curve often bouncing off the old tires that formed the outer boundaries. On the fifth turn, Sarah passed her and quickly gained a healthy lead. She felt a rush of joy as she looked back at Jessica. She was laughing as she rocked back and forth urging her car to go faster.

When the lap counter clicked off the fourteenth lap, Sarah pulled into the pit and waited. Jessica quickly pulled up beside her. "That was so much fun. This is wonderful!" She leaned over and grabbed Sarah's hand. "If I forget to tell you later, I had a great time." They both laughed. "Now that I have a feel for the track, I'm ready to win. Start thinking about what time you need to get up to get my coffee ready."

"Whatever."

"The race starts as soon as the first person gets to the start line," Jessica yelled as she jetted out in front once again.

"You cheat!" Sarah yelled at her.

They whipped around the track again. Jessica had a huge lead and was not slowing as much on the corners this time. Sarah had no chance of catching her. When Jessica crossed the finish line after lap fourteen, she didn't stop at the pit. Instead she went all the way around and stopped at the start line waiting for Sarah to catch up.

Sarah came around the last corner and started protesting before she even came to a stop. "You cheat. That was not a fair race." She pretended to be really mad, but couldn't keep from smiling. "You're so competitive. I'm glad I'm not one of your business competitors."

"Show no mercy," she yelled as she hit the gas again.

"Dang it!"

The final race ended with Jessica maintaining the tiny lead throughout all fourteen laps. She laughed an evil victory laugh as she finished.

They brought the cars to a stop near the other cars and flannel-shirt man was there waiting. "I'll get those for you girls. Did you have a good time?"

Jessica got out of her car and gave him a quick hug. "I had the best time. Thank you so much."

"No, thank you." He laughed loudly. "It's truly rare to get a hug in my job especially from such a beautiful young lady. Don't go gettin' no ideas though, cause my wife is at that counter over there." He smiled at her and pointed across the track.

"It's her first time out of the big city." Sarah laughed at Jessica, who was normally so cool and reserved.

"Why don't you girls go get you an ice cream on the house, and play some skee ball while you're in the arcade? It's still all clear of the kids."

"Ice cream sounds good." Jessica looked anxiously at Sarah. "But I don't know what skeet ball is."

"Well, tonight is full of firsts then. You surely did lead a sheltered childhood—no skee ball?"

"Show me. I'm sure I can beat you at that too," Jessica said and grabbed Sarah's hand. They walked hand in hand to the arcade and got their ice cream from Mrs. Flannel-Shirt.

"Okay, so what you do is roll the ball so it goes into those holes up there in the top. The more points you get the more little tickets pop out here." Sarah leaned over and showed Jessica the slot at the end of the machine. "Then you take your tickets and get yourself one of those fancy prizes." She pointed to the rack of cheap, plastic toys over the counter.

"You're kidding me? You earn prizes from playing the game?" Jessica was grinning again. "I love prizes. Let's play."

"I'll get some tokens." She put her money in the machine and returned with several tokens.

Sarah inserted a token in two machines side by side and a dozen skee balls dropped down on each.

"Shall I show you?"

"No. I got this." Jessica threw the ball overhanded at the top of the alley, and it bounced off hard and went flying across the room.

"Jess! You're going to get us killed, or at least thrown out of this fancy joint." Sarah laughed. "You roll it up. Don't throw it." Jessica laughed too. "Good thing no one else was in here; you could have hit them in the head." They both laughed like a couple of teenage girls. Sarah rolled all her balls one at a time and hit the center circle ten out of twelve times. Jessica looked in awe as the tickets clicked out in mass.

"Wow! Show me how you did that."

"Pick up one of the balls." Sarah wrapped her left arm around Jessica's petite waist and took her right hand, which was holding the ball. She felt the warmth of Jessica's body and sensed the familiar flutter in her stomach. "You feel good."

"Hmm, I think I really like learning how to throw a skeet ball."

Sarah laughed and pulled her closer. "*Skee* ball my sexy, sheltered girl." She drew her arm back and launched her arm forward, but Jessica released too late, and the ball went flying in the air. They both ducked and laughed again when the ball thudded on the floor. Sarah spun Jessica around and kissed her long and deep. They quickly backed away from each other at the sound of the bell on the door, and watched two teenage boys stroll in.

Sarah whispered in Jessica's ear. "Let's go practice something else and learn skee ball another day."

"Excellent idea," Jessica said. "I think I might be a little better at the new game you're suggesting."

"I'd say." Sarah licked her lips.

"Hey, if you guys want this game and these tickets, they're all yours," Sarah said to the boys. They just stared at her.

Sarah started pulling Jessica toward the door. "Time to move along. We're actually right near my house." They ran out the door and across the parking lot toward the truck. They both jumped in, and Sarah had the truck on the road in seconds. Jessica didn't say a word, but started unbuttoning Sarah's five-button jeans as she drove toward her house.

"You're going to get us killed. What are you, seventeen?"

Jessica kissed Sarah's neck and put her hand over her crotch. "You make me feel like it. I had a wonderful time tonight. I have so much fun with you. You make me so happy."

"Yeah," was all she said as she squirmed while Jessica tried to maneuver her hand into Sarah's pants. They pulled in the drive within minutes. Jessica jumped out and grabbed Sarah. She stopped long enough to kiss her, slipping her tongue across Sarah's teeth.

"Do you need to call Jimmy for a ride tomorrow?"

"I already told him to pick me up at eight in the morning." Jessica blushed a little and quickly changed the subject. "Remember, I want my coffee in bed before he arrives."

"You're pretty demanding." Sarah pushed her against the door as she closed it and began to unbutton Jessica's Levi's. They moved slowly toward the bedroom tangled in each other's clothes.

Jimmy was right on time. Sarah met him with coffee as Jessica finished dressing.

"Thank you for the best night of my life." Jessica leaned in to kiss her and hesitated a minute. "I have to work late tonight.

I promised my partners I would connect for a conference call when I got finished today."

"Oh yeah, of course. You came here to work. I've been consuming all your time."

"Don't be silly. I want to spend time with you. I *love* spending time with you. I could call you later when I'm done, and maybe you could come by."

"Ah...maybe it's a good idea for us to take a break. I have some work I need to do as well," Sarah said.

"I'm the one who's been keeping you from work. You're right. I'll wait to hear from you."

Sarah began shutting down immediately. "Yeah, I'll call." She imagined never calling, curling up with Benny, and asking Cheryl to forgive her, reminding herself that the love of her life had died.

❖

"How was your evening, Ms. Whitney?" Jimmy asked as they drove to the hotel.

Jessica looked in the mirror. "It was amazing. We rode go-karts."

"Excuse me, ma'am, but did you say you rode go-karts?"

Jessica laughed. "Yes, Jimmy, I did. We always have so much fun together. I don't know why she pushes me away."

"Maybe she's scared of a relationship with a rich, beautiful woman."

"Why does everything have to be about money?"

Jimmy laughed and then looked in the mirror. "Ms. Whitney, you know how much I love you, and I mean no disrespect, but, ma'am, you have no idea. Money is only a big deal when you don't have it."

Jessica knew Sarah was struggling financially right now, and that probably made it easy to target her wealth. She wished there was something she could do. She would gladly pay any amount of money to help Sarah out. She was sure whatever the amount—it would be insignificant to her, but she knew Sarah wouldn't let her. Sarah would be insulted if she even offered. "What can I do?"

"Nothing, ma'am. Just be patient with her and care about her the way you always do."

"Maybe I could figure out how to help her out without her knowing it was me."

"No, ma'am. You shouldn't do that."

Jessica looked up at him. She knew he was right. She hated that she had so much and would gladly give it to Sarah, but she would never take it.

CHAPTER ELEVEN

Sarah managed another productive day. She got three jewelry boxes cut out and ready for construction. When she found a good stopping place, she locked the shop and dusted off the sawdust that covered her from head to toe. She had been in the shop since Jessica left, only stopping occasionally for a bathroom break and to fill her water bottle. Once inside, she headed straight for the shower. It was dark already, but she had forgotten to look at a clock before she got in the shower. It felt late, but in the fall, the early darkness confused her internal clock. She wondered if she would hear from Jessica tonight. She really wanted her here, but maybe it was best if they had a break. Things were moving quickly, and where were they going—there was no place for them to go.

Sarah finished her shower and sat in her recliner. She was wrapped in only her cotton robe. She fell asleep almost as soon as she sat down.

At seven, Sarah felt the cool dampness of Benny's nose on her hand. It was chow time, and she was impatient when it came to chow. Sarah patted her on the head, "Hungry, ol' girl?" Benny ran to her bowl and sat down as Sarah poured the dry food in the bowl. Benny sat looking at the food waiting to be told she could begin. Sarah was so focused on her thoughts that she almost forgot to tell her to eat. "Okay, girl, eat up."

Sarah left Benny to her quick task and went to her room. She dug through the basket of clean clothes sitting in front of her closet and pulled on some shorts and a T-shirt. At her computer, she opened up some old designs to work on tomorrow and considered dinner, but the thought of eating alone just didn't feel good. She wondered if she should call Jessica. She wanted to, but didn't want to. When she was with her all she wanted was to be close to her and know her better. Jessica was such an amazing woman, but when she had too much time to think, she felt guilty as if she were betraying Cheryl, and she put up defenses to protect her heart. After nearly an hour, she gave in and punched up Jessica's number already saved in her phone.

"Hello!" Jessica answered.

"What are you doing?"

"I'm sitting here staring at my computer wishing you would call—how about you?"

"Your wish just came true. I'm sitting here wishing I had something to eat and someone to enjoy it with me."

"Shall I come get you? We can go grab something. I'm starving too. In fact, I can't remember eating today."

"Jess, seriously. That's so bad for you."

"Well...did you eat?"

"Okay, fine. You got me. How about we grab some takeout and eat here? I don't feel like going out, and I like you in my house."

"Hmm, I like it there. What if I pick something up on the way over?" Jessica offered.

"You don't mind?"

"Of course not. What sounds good?"

"Anything. Oh, except Chinese."

"That will be easy to remember. I don't care for Chinese either. Okay, give me an hour or so," Jessica said.

❖

The bell rang and Benny repeated the announcement with her single bark and trotted to the door with Sarah in tow.

They greeted Jessica and Jimmy. They both held bags stuffed with Styrofoam food containers.

Jessica leaned in to kiss her, and Jimmy backed up quickly. "Ms. Sarah, I didn't know you had a dog."

"Jimmy, she won't hurt you. Please come in."

They both came in, and Jessica headed for the kitchen. Jimmy followed giving Benny a wide berth. Benny just looked at him since Sarah had not released her. He set the bags of food on the table.

"What did you guys do, bring the whole menu?" Sarah looked at all the food.

"Well, yes, actually. I didn't know what you would like, and the hotel was pleased to prepare whatever I wanted." Jessica smiled.

"Ms. Whitney, if that's all, I'll be going now," Jimmy said quietly.

Sarah caught him. "Jimmy, you'll pick her up in the morning, right?"

He looked over at Jessica. "Ma'am?"

"Yes, Jimmy. Same time as today." Jessica smiled at him.

"Yes, ma'am," he said as he disappeared through the front door.

Sarah turned to Benny. "It's okay now. Silly men are scared of you—come here." She rubbed her head. "You're a good girl." She returned to the table. "Seriously, Jess, what are we going to do with all this food?"

"We'll have leftovers—for a long time. Let's eat."

Sarah sighed scanning the dozen boxes on the table. They sat at the table and began opening boxes.

❖

They barely got the food put away before Sarah had her hands up Jessica's tight white T-shirt caressing her full breasts. Jessica gave in quickly and pulled her to the bedroom. They may have gotten a bit more sleep, but the sound of Jimmy's call still came too early.

Sarah moved a little more slowly today, but she managed to have the coffee ready when Jimmy arrived. This was becoming a routine that while having a negative impact on her sleep pattern, she was enjoying very much. Some nights, they lay in each other's arms in the afterglow of their lovemaking talking and laughing for hours.

Sarah shared much of her past, but still never got close to the subject of Cheryl. She was beginning to feel like it would be weird now. Too much time had passed. It would be like correcting someone for calling you by the wrong name weeks after they first made the mistake. Not only did she not want to talk about it, now it would be really awkward. Jessica would probably wonder why she hadn't mentioned her deceased partner.

Sarah had spent so long alone in her house—just her and Benny—she didn't even realize how lonely she was. As long as

Jessica was there, Sarah was happy. Each morning when Jessica drove away, that wave of guilt hit her. How could she love someone else? Cheryl was the only one—her true soul mate.

Jessica was so different from her. She was rich. Was that the only thing that made her different? It seemed like so much more, but they had so much in common. Jessica didn't seem to notice that Sarah had no money. She seemed to embrace Sarah's simple life, and even wanted to meet her friends. Sarah was falling in love with her. It was clear to her even when she pushed the thoughts away. Jessica would be gone soon, and this constant struggle would be over. It was a thought she relished and feared at the same time.

During the day, they both fell quickly into their routines. The loss of sleep was taking a toll on both of them. Sarah came in and took a quick nap most afternoons, losing valuable shop time, but she was hoping to avoid losing a finger. She knew how unsafe it was to work out there when she wasn't rested and she was getting behind.

❖

Jessica had never been so happy. She had never known a woman she felt this way about before. She couldn't get enough of her, talking to her, dining with her, go-kart riding with her, sharing ideas with her, and of course making love with her. She knew she was falling for Sarah, and she even occasionally let her mind wander—dreaming of a life they could share together. She would buy them a big beautiful home and make Sarah's workshop even bigger. It was a nice dream.

She hoped to be brave enough to tell Sarah how she felt soon. She wanted to now, but she was confused by Sarah. Most of the time they spent together was perfect, but sometimes Sarah kept a little distance. Jessica was sure there was something she didn't know. There were occasionally strange moments of silence and times when she knew she was being directed away from a subject. She didn't want to express her feelings until she was sure Sarah felt the same way.

Jessica started another day of meetings and coordinating projects from long distance. Most days she didn't mind that her caffeine consumption had increased dramatically just to help her make it through the long meetings. She realized that they couldn't keep up this pace much longer, but neither of them wanted to miss out on their evenings together.

Jessica was sending Jimmy home for Thanksgiving, and she was taking him to the airport for a late flight tonight. Perhaps tonight would be a good night to try to catch up on her sleep. She wanted to be with Sarah, but she would spend the whole day with her tomorrow. She'd give her a call.

❖

"Hello." Sarah tried to sound awake. She had just dozed off in her recliner with Benny on top of her. Benny occasionally thought she was a lap dog.

"Were you asleep?"

"No...no I was just taking a little break," she fibbed.

"You were sleeping! I caught you."

"Yeah, you caught me. What are you doing?" Sarah asked.

"Well, I wanted to talk to you about tonight." She paused. "I have to take Jimmy to the airport tonight. He's going back to Chicago to spend Thanksgiving with his family. He wanted to come right back on Friday morning, but I'm actually not going to be able to do much here until next Monday. Seems people around here like their holidays and time off, so I'll just work in the hotel on Friday and the rest of the weekend. I thought I'd just stay here tonight, and I could come by tomorrow and pick you up for our Thanksgiving dinner."

Sarah felt a pang of disappointment in her chest. She knew she occasionally kept her distance, but she had been working hard not to push Jessica away. She wondered if she had failed, or was Jessica doing the pushing this time? Things had been great—amazing in fact. "Jess, did I do something wrong?"

"No! Sarah, you've done everything right. It's just...I need some sleep. You're killing me."

Sarah burst out laughing. "What are you, the old lady here?"

"Oh no, you don't! You're taking a nap. Do you do that every day? Besides, I don't want to be a zombie when I meet your friends tomorrow. The sex will be written all over us."

Sarah laughed again. "That's a story we shouldn't be ashamed to tell. They'll just be jealous. Seriously, come over here tonight, and we can just sleep. In fact, that sounds nice. I could even heat up the Jacuzzi, and we could sit and soak with a glass of wine." Sarah felt a bit of remorse about the hot tub. She should get one more use out of it. She had an offer on it and was going to drain it so she could sell it this weekend. It would help with the expenses, and she didn't use it much anymore. She and Cheryl had spent nearly every Friday evening in it during the winter months.

"As nice as that sounds, I don't trust that we'll actually sleep, especially if we spend time soaking naked in a hot tub. I know I won't be able to keep my hands off you, and based on the events of last night, you apparently have no self-control either."

"You have a point, but really. Don't stay in that hotel. Come over. We'll have something to eat. You may recall my refrigerator is full of leftovers. We'll each go put on pajamas, and we'll crawl in bed with the TV on until we fall asleep. How's that for unromantic? Nothing like a TV to ruin the mood, right? The only thing less romantic would be if I had a video game." She chuckled.

"Well, okay. I do want to see you. I'll be there a bit late. Jimmy's flight is not until eight. He'll be getting home so late. I tried to get him to leave earlier. I think he fibbed to me and told me it was the only flight Mattie could get for him. I insisted on driving him to the airport. He agreed only if I would just drop him at the curb, so I'll be there soon after."

"Wait, can you even drive?" Sarah asked seriously.

"Yes, of course. I can't help that my first car was a limo. I made Jimmy teach me about five years ago. He still teases me, but I drive quite well, thank you very much."

"Okay. I'll see you tonight. Mind if I eat before you get here?"

"No, you should. I'll pick up a salad or something before I leave. See you." Jessica clicked off.

Sarah looked at her watch and decided she had better get back to work.

❖

"Please tell Natalie I said happy Thanksgiving," Jessica said to Jimmy as he was pulling into the departure drop-off lane.

"I'm excited to see her. It's been since August. She grows so much every time I see her. I hardly recognize her as my little girl anymore." Jimmy pulled over to the curb and held the door as Jessica got out and climbed in the driver side. "You know where you're going, right?"

"Yes, Jimmy. I know where I'm going," she said.

"The traffic should be light this time of day, but her exit is a little busy at the intersection off the highway, remember."

"Jimmy, quit worrying. You're going to miss your flight."

"Okay. Thank you, Ms. Whitney. I'll see you in a couple days." Jimmy climbed out and closed the door.

"You're not supposed to return until Monday," Jessica said quickly as the door slammed shut.

Jimmy looked in the window and winked.

"Dammit, Jimmy," she said, but his back was turned to her and he walked away.

Jessica adjusted the seat and mirror and took a big deep breath before she drove out of the airport and headed in the direction of Sarah's house. After she drove for nearly twenty minutes, she realized she was going the wrong way on the highway. She cursed herself out loud. "You are so spoiled. You can't even drive to a location you've been to a half dozen times in less than a week."

She reached for the cell phone in her purse as she drove farther out of the way waiting for the next exit. Her phone wasn't there. She knew immediately where it was. It was sitting on the desk in the hotel where she had left it when she changed earlier. Jimmy was always scolding her for forgetting her phone.

After driving for another ten minutes, she exited the highway and turned around. She was even more confused about where she was so she took the first familiar exit and found herself downtown. The good news was she recognized the hotel and was sure she could get to Sarah's from there.

Aside from go-karts, Jessica hated driving. She never told anyone just how much she hated it. She was teased enough about always having a chauffeur. She drove up and down one-way streets in downtown Phoenix for several minutes before she finally got back to the hotel. After she spun around in the parking lot, she headed toward Sarah's house. She hoped. Why couldn't she remember a single landmark? She felt like she was in a city she had never visited before. Jessica finally saw the highway sign and knew she was heading the right way. Once on the highway, she knew she was home free. Or so she thought. She exited too early and didn't realize it until she had driven up and down neighborhood streets looking for Sarah's house for almost thirty minutes.

Finally back on the highway, she spotted the right exit. The congestion Jimmy was worried about was long gone by the time she got there, but she did recognize it because Jimmy had made a comment about the construction work causing a backup the other day. Everything was familiar again, and soon she saw Sarah's house and her big truck beside it. She was so late. Sarah was going to kill her—so much for relaxing and getting a good night's sleep.

Sarah opened the door, relieved to see Jessica there. It was after ten. "I was so worried about you. What happened? What took you so long? Why didn't you answer your phone? Why didn't you call?"

Jessica walked in the house and patted Benny who was waiting patiently in her spot. "I got lost," she said and flushed red.

"Jess, you've been here almost every night for a week. How did you get lost?"

"Jimmy drives, I sit in the back, and well…I don't know what it is I do really. I just don't pay attention to where he is going."

"GPS? Cell phone? This is the twenty-first century. Ten more minutes and I was going to call the police. You scared the shit out of me."

"This rental doesn't have GPS, and I forgot my phone. I'm sorry. I knew you would be worried."

Sarah was still angry from having worried so much. The fear that had consumed her while she paced through her house was a familiar agony. "Seriously…rich girls!" She shook her head. "How the fuck do you manage?"

Jessica jerked back and stared at Sarah. Then she spoke through gritted teeth. "I manage quite fine. Have you not noticed my multi-fucking-million dollar company? What's up your ass? I said I was sorry."

Jessica standing up for herself took the fire out of Sarah. "Damn, girl. You don't take any shit, do you?" She pulled her in for a hug. "I'm sorry. I was just worried and scared. I hate to be scared."

Jessica was stiff, not responding to Sarah's embrace. She knew she was still reacting to the stinging words, but slowly, Jessica began to relax into Sarah's strong arms and returned the hug.

Jessica backed away and held Sarah's hands. "Please don't make money more than it is."

"You're right. I'm sorry. My words were mean and hurtful. Forgive me for yelling like an idiot." Sarah pulled Jessica close to her again.

"Okay, I forgive you. I'm sorry I scared you."

"Good." She hugged her tighter and took in her clean smell before she led her to the bedroom.

"I thought we had a sleeping deal tonight." Jessica followed.

"Yes, and I have laid out some pajamas for you. I'm going to let Benny out one more time and lock up. That will give you time to change and then I'll be back in a minute."

"You're an excellent planner."

Jessica pulled on the pajama pants and a too large gray Air Force R.O.T.C T-shirt and climbed into Sarah's bed.

Sarah turned on her music as she passed through the living room. Damien Rice was singing "Cannonball," softly coming from the small speakers placed discreetly behind the bed.

She let Benny out the back and checked the shop door, which was part of her regular routine. Benny followed Sarah back in after taking care of her business. Sarah locked the front door as she headed back to the bedroom, and Benny took her post at the door. Sarah looked at her and felt the twinge of pain. "Why don't you sleep in here with us tonight, ol' girl?" But Benny only looked up at her and didn't move.

Sarah returned to the bedroom and went straight to the bathroom. "I'll be right out." Sarah changed into the pajamas she had put in the bathroom. She came out and turned off all the lights and quickly climbed in bed.

"I was hoping if I put you in a baggy T-shirt I wouldn't be so tempted to caress your beautiful breasts, but somehow it isn't working." Sarah leaned in and kissed her.

Jessica looked at her and yawned. "Tell me about your family," she asked out of nowhere.

"Well, that short, very boring story will put you to sleep in just a few minutes." Sarah rubbed Jessica's shoulders. "Roll over and I'll rub your back until you fall asleep."

"I won't turn down a back rub, but I want you to tell me about your family while you do it."

"Okay. I'll tell you, but honestly, there's not much to tell."
Sarah rolled over to her nightstand and put lotion on her hands.
She rubbed them together to warm the lotion before she placed
her hands on Jessica's back. "I've already told you all there
really is to know. I'm from a small town in Illinois. My whole
family is still there. My dad was a carpenter. He worked for the
local farmers remodeling kitchens and bathrooms or building
hog sheds."

"Hog sheds, really?" Jessica asked.

"Yep, that's what farmers need. He died of leukemia while
I was in college. I have—"

Jessica interrupted. "I'm sorry. I didn't know your dad had
passed."

"Yeah, thank you. I miss him most when I build something
I would like to show him. The sad thing is, I didn't realize what
an impression he had made on me and who I am until he was
gone, but I know he would be proud of me."

"Of course he would be. There's a lot to be proud of,
Colonel."

"You're funny. You keep that up, and I'll start making you
salute me."

"Go on. Tell me more."

"Well, my mom, who is still alive and well, was a secretary.
I was a latchkey kid, but I never minded. I didn't know it was
supposed to be any different. I do remember really liking it
when my mom took vacation time during the school year and
was at the house when I got home. They divorced when I was in
seventh grade, but it wasn't too bad because they lived just down
the street from one another. I'd just go back and forth whenever I
wanted. If I didn't like what Mom was having for supper I went
to Dad's. I had a pretty great stepdad, quiet and nonintrusive, but

always there. I have an older sister and an older brother, both are still in Illinois, both have been married to the same person for a very long time, and they both have kids. That's it." Sarah continued to rub Jessica's back. "Did I put you to sleep?"

"No, it sounds nice."

"It was. I like where I came from, and my family is close. It is a little weird. We don't hug much or often tell each other, but we all love each other, and we all know it. It's kind of understood. I know it sounds weird, right?"

"It sounds comforting and safe."

"What about you? I know about Daddy wanting a lawyer. What about your mom?"

"My mom died of cancer, also."

"Oh geez, Jess. I'm sorry." Sarah put her arms around Jessica and squeezed.

"It's okay. I hardly knew her. I hadn't seen her in years."

"You don't have to tell me if you don't want to."

"No, I don't mind. Because Mom was black, she never felt like she was accepted by the Whitney family, but I sometimes wonder if she wanted a reason to hate them."

"I didn't know you were biracial." Sarah caught herself. "But why would I?"

"I guess I assumed you knew. Does it matter?"

"Of course not." Sarah rubbed Jessica's lower back and thighs. "Go on, tell me."

"Well, my parents met at DePaul University, and the way I hear it they were madly in love. I never saw that. I only ever saw them fight. They divorced after my tenth birthday. My mother moved back to Indiana. She said she tried to get custody of me, but Gramps wouldn't let me go. The Whitneys pretty much get what they want. You've been victim of that."

"Who's a victim? I consider myself a survivor."

"I used to feel abandoned by her. I thought she didn't love me. I would see her once or twice a year, and it was always difficult because we didn't know each other. I remember one visit on my twelfth birthday. All I wanted for my birthday was to spend time with my mom. Her limo driver picked me up at the airport and when he dropped me off at the house I ran in to see her. Her maid, Sonya, pointed me toward my bedroom, and I was so excited thinking she was in my room to surprise me. When I swung the door open, I saw the room was filled floor to ceiling with brightly wrapped boxes and balloons with a big paper sign that said happy birthday. There were more presents than most kids would get their whole lives, but my mother wasn't there.

"I didn't open a single one. I guess she took them all back. I just waited for her at the front door until late at night. Sonya finally carried me to bed. My mom didn't come home until two days later and my visit ended the next day. She thought giving presents was the way to show love."

"Wow, that sucks."

"Yeah. I was still in high school when I came out to her. She told me she didn't want to see me anymore. Now I try not to think about her. And my dad, well, I haven't talked to him in close to three years, and I have no siblings." Jessica finished her story just as Cher finished belting out "Love Hurts." "Leave it to Cher to sum it up so nicely," Jessica laughed.

"Jess…" Sarah didn't know what to say so she wrapped her arms tightly around Jessica's body.

"Sorry that was a bit of a downer. It's okay though. I have a great family. Everyone at work is my family, and I love taking care of them."

"Who takes care of you?" Sarah whispered in her ear.

"I don't really need anything."

"Hmm, okay."

John Mayer started with "Your Body is a Wonderland," and Jessica rolled over to kiss Sarah. "Let's see if we can improve the mood in here and take Mr. Mayer's advice because I think your body is a wonderland."

"I thought you wanted to sleep." Sarah kissed her, deep and hungry, feeling the heat of Jessica's body pushed tightly against her.

"You know we do get to sleep in tomorrow, don't you?" Jessica reminded her.

Jessica pulled Sarah on top of her and they kissed. Within moments, pajamas had been tossed over the edge of the bed. "Best laid plans…" Jessica breathed in Sarah's ear. They made love, and then lay in each other's arms listening to Sarah's never-ending playlist and talking softly until they fell asleep.

❖

Sarah woke to the nudge of Benny's cold nose. It was after nine, and Benny had waited patiently as long as she could. Jessica lay next to her with her head on Sarah's shoulder and her leg across her. It felt so nice. She let Benny out and snuggled back in bed with her for a few more hours.

Sarah had been awake since she let Benny out, just dozing a little and enjoying the warmth of Jessica next to her. She refused to think about anything but Jessica. She finally kissed her gently on the forehead. She had barely moved all night. "Jess, it's almost noon. We should probably think about getting ready."

Jessica stirred a little and raised her head to look at Sarah. "It can't be noon. I don't think I've ever slept until noon in my whole rich life." She yawned and looked at Sarah.

"Well, my beautiful rich girl," Sarah teased back. "You did today."

"You're serious. Wow!" She laid her head back across Sarah's chest. "That's what you do to me. You have totally exhausted me."

"And you love every minute of it." Sarah tickled her a little.

"Oh you think so, do you?" She tried to tickle her back, but Sarah gripped both arms and flipped her over. After wrestling and making out for a few minutes, Sarah pulled Jessica out of bed and into the shower.

CHAPTER TWELVE

In the truck driving over to Patricia and Christine's, Jessica begged for information. "Tell me about Patricia and Christine. Will they like me? What did you tell them about me?" Jessica had been asking questions and acting antsy since they got out of the shower.

"What is wrong with you? You're supposed to be the calm, cool, power woman executive. You act like you're scared of my friends. They're just two nice lesbians."

"Are you kidding? I'm scared to death of those two nice lesbians. If they don't like me, I'm screwed. I never care if the business people I work with like me or not. In fact, it's often better if they don't."

"Well, I have no sympathy," Sarah said as she climbed out of her truck. "You're the one who agreed to this."

"You're no help. When I go into an executive meeting I always have my staff prepare me with some good information about who I'm meeting with." They were nearing the door. "What do you have for me?" she asked, rushing her question as they approached the house.

"I have only one piece of advice for you. Don't get trapped alone with Christine!" The door opened and Patricia and Christine enveloped them both in hugs.

"It's about time you got here," Patricia said to Sarah and then she whispered in her ear. "Did you guys have sex all night again?"

Sarah gave her an evil look. "Wouldn't you like to know?"

"I knew it," Patricia said out loud. Sarah poked her in the side.

"Patricia, Christine, this is Jessica. Jess, these crazy ladies are my dearest friends. This is Patricia, and this is Christine." Sarah gestured to each.

Patricia embraced Jessica again. "It is so nice to finally meet you. We can barely get this one to tell us anything." Patricia pointed her finger at Sarah.

Christine took her turn with a hug and started asking questions. "So you're an architect? Sarah tells us you're putting up a large commercial office building downtown. Where is it going? Who's putting it up?"

"It's already beginning." Sarah patted Jessica on the shoulder and turned to Christine. "Give her a chance to breathe now and then, will you? I'll go help Patti finish up."

Jessica gave her a look of desperation.

"You'll be fine. She's mostly harmless. I'll bring you a drink." Sarah and Patricia walked to the kitchen and left Jessica with Christine.

When Sarah returned, Christine and Jessica were sitting comfortably in the living room. Jessica was explaining the details of the new building, and Christine appeared to be hanging on every word.

"Wow. I don't think I've ever seen her stop the third degree long enough for someone to actually get a chance to answer her," Sarah said.

Christine frowned at Sarah. "Has she told you about this building? It sounds amazing."

"She has. It is going to be amazing." She sat next to Jessica. Sarah gave her a glass of wine and kissed her cheek.

"Is the firm your family's business?" Christine tried again.

"No," Jessica calmly answered. "I have two partners. We started it from the ground up with a gift from my grandfather about fifteen years ago. We've been incredibly lucky."

"Luck has nothing to do with it. You are good!" Sarah said.

"Thank you so much." She kissed Sarah. "I do think there was a little luck involved, and Grandpa's name didn't hurt either."

"Oh, was your grandpa famous?" Christine asked.

Patricia returned. "Chris, give the woman a break. Besides, everyone come in and give me a hand getting the food on the table. It's ready."

"It smells wonderful, Patricia." Jessica jumped up first to help or to run from Christine's questions. Sarah wasn't quite sure which. "Your home is beautifully decorated."

Christine spoke up. "It should be. We had it done by the best decorator in town." She kissed Patricia.

"Really? I'll need a good decorator for the top floor executive offices. Does your decorator do commercial work?"

They laughed at her and Sarah spoke up. "Chris, your joke is only funny if she knows Patricia is a decorator."

"You did all this? It's really wonderful." Jessica quickly caught on. "Do you work on commercial projects?"

"I work on any project. Remind me to give you my card after dinner." Jessica moved next to Sarah and wrapped her arms around her. "You didn't tell me anything about your friends."

"Sorry." Sarah smiled and slipped away.

They all shuffled around the kitchen as Patricia choreographed the process, and soon they all surrounded the table in the large dining room. Patricia lit the candles.

"Okay, sit everyone," Patricia said. The table was covered with food including all the standard Thanksgiving fare: turkey, stuffing, potatoes, yams, green beans, and several salads.

"Everything looks great, honey." Christine winked at Patricia from across the table as they all took their seats.

"Don't let her make you think I did this all myself. She helped with everything."

Patricia fussed over everyone, making sure they had all the food their plate could possibly hold and finally settled in to fill her own plate. "Eat, ladies. Don't wait."

"Oh, this turkey is so moist and tender and the stuffing is amazing. Thank you so much for inviting me," Jessica said between bites. "I can't remember the last time I had a traditional Thanksgiving dinner."

"What do you normally do for Thanksgiving?" Christine asked.

"I left myself open for that question, didn't I? I often travel during the holidays."

"You don't spend time with family?"

"Christine!" Patricia said. "I can dress her up, but I can't take her anywhere."

"It's okay. My father is my only living family, and he and I don't see eye to eye on, well, anything. He wanted a boy to take over his law firm, not a lesbian architect." She frowned.

Sarah found Jessica's foot under the table with her own foot. "So, Chris, how's the case load?" It was the perfect distraction. Christine discussed the details of several of her cases through the remainder of dinner. After they finished the meal, they took their wine to the living room.

With an empty wine bottle in her hand Sarah said, "Ladies, have we really finished four bottles of wine? I think this is the last one."

Patricia looked at Christine. "You've been drinking all the wine."

"I'm not the only one." Christine pointed back at Patricia

"Whatever. I'm going to clear some of these dishes. Are you going to challenge our guests to some Trivial Pursuit?" Patricia looked at Christine.

"Oh no, please, not today. I'm sick of getting my ass kicked by you," Sarah whined.

"Let's play teams." Jessica stood up. "Don't worry, Sarah. We got this. I'm quite good at trivia." She followed Patricia in the kitchen with some dishes.

"You guys get the game set up. We'll straighten up a bit," Patricia said.

Sarah turned to Christine. "Oh, you're in for it now. My girl is good."

Jessica carried a load of dishes into the kitchen. "Thank you so much for having me today. It has been a great day."

Patricia reached over and hugged her, and then turned back to the sink to rinse dishes for Jessica to put in the dishwasher. "You've been so good for her. I can see how much you both care for one another. I'm sure she has told you what an impact losing Cheryl has been. Your being around has been so good for her. Just be careful. She's still pretty wounded, and those wounds still bleed sometimes."

Jessica stopped and stood staring at Patricia, speechless.

Patricia turned to hand Jessica a dish and stopped, holding the dish between them. "Oh no, she didn't tell—I'm such an idiot. We were all so comfortable out there, I just, oh, I've put you in a difficult situation, and Sarah is going to kill me. If you decide to tell her I told you then I understand, but if it would be easier to wait until she tells you, well, I get that too. I'll just stop talking now."

"Patricia, who's Cheryl? You're in it now. Please tell me. Is she why Sarah keeps a wedge between us most of the time?"

"Listen, I've screwed up and now isn't the time—unless you want this day to get really bad really quickly. I'll tell you that Cheryl was her wife of fifteen years, and she was a narcotics detective killed in action. Please, the last thing I want to do is hurt her or betray her trust. I'll stall them. Go get yourself together. You'll need to process this later. Please."

Jessica nodded and went to the bathroom. Pretty soon, Jessica returned. "Can I call you and talk about this and what I should do?"

Patricia nodded. "For now, put on your happy face, and let's play some trivia." Jessica walked behind her to the living room.

❖

It was late when they finally got back to Sarah's house, and for the first time since they'd known each other, they both went right to sleep with barely a word.

When Jessica woke up, she could tell before even rolling over that she was alone in the bed. In the week and half since they'd been sleeping together, rarely was there a moment when they weren't touching, and now Sarah wasn't there. She rolled over and saw 7:57 on the digital clock in the corner and a piece of paper on Sarah's pillow. "Come get me in the shop when you wake up. I'll fix breakfast." At the bottom of the page was an eerie authentic looking drawing of a small hand with a finger missing and beside it the words, "Wait to come in if you hear tools running."

Jessica stopped at the front hall closet as she headed for the shop. She grabbed Sarah's thick Carhartt jacket and pulled it on. It smelled of wood and a hint of Sarah's sweet fragrance. She inhaled the memory-evoking scent and felt a sense of melancholy as she remembered her short discussion with Patricia. She stood outside the door of the shop listening, and the only thing she heard was the click of Benny's toenails on the concrete floor. Benny had heard her come out of the house and was waiting for her to enter. She slowly opened the door and scanned the large space. Finally, she spotted Sarah. She sat on her workbench with her legs swinging back and forth, staring off into space.

"Hey, are you okay?" Jessica had never seen her so distant and distracted.

Sarah turned abruptly at the sound of her voice. She stared blankly for a moment and then jumped off the table and trotted over to her as if it finally registered who was there. "Good morning, beautiful," she said as she embraced her. "I wanted to let you sleep in." She glanced at her watch. "You didn't make it too long."

"I missed you in the bed. Are you sure you're okay?"

"Yeah...I...I was just working through a design problem. Want some breakfast?" Sarah moved them both toward the door.

"Ahh...Sarah. I want to talk to you."

"That doesn't sound good. Let's go in the house. There's still a chill in here."

They crossed the patio back into the house. Sarah poured a cup of coffee for Jessica and refilled her own. Jessica just stood staring at her. "Do you want to sit down?"

"Yes." Jessica took the seat at the table where she sat each night when they ate dinner together.

"What is it?" Sarah said, sounding impatient.

"Sarah, I know about Cheryl," she blurted it out not knowing what else to do.

Sarah's already gloomy expression sank. "Patti told you?"

"Please don't be mad at Patricia. She thought I already knew. She was taking care of you, protecting you from any pain I might cause you. She's concerned you will hate her for this."

"No one could hate Patti. I owe her and Christine so much. I wouldn't have made it without them. I don't hate her." She was staring at the table playing with a knot hole in the surface. "Are you planning to hurt me?"

"What? No, I don't want to hurt you." Jessica looked at her. She was still not meeting her eyes. "She didn't tell me any details, only that she had passed." Jessica reached for Sarah's hand. Sarah didn't move or react. "Oh, sweetheart, I'm so sorry. Why didn't you tell me?"

"Jess, do you mind if I spend some time alone today—maybe the rest of the weekend?" Sarah didn't look up.

"Is that what you want?" She tilted her head down to try to see Sarah's eyes. "Are you upset that I know?"

She raised her head. Her eyes were clear but vacant. "No, I'm not upset. I suppose I should have told you. I didn't know really what was going on with us. It just seemed too complicated for the fun we were having."

Jessica's heart sank. Is that all this had been for her, fun sex? Yes, it had started that way and maybe she hadn't even expected much more, but there was more now. She felt it, and she knew Sarah felt it too—if she would only let herself.

"I think I need a break from everything. This project is just not coming together, and it's costing me as much as I'm going to make on it. I'm so far behind I'll never get the bonus I was promised. I need some space from us. I think I'll just pack it in for the day and take Benny up to the foothills for a hike. I'll breathe in some fresh air and stop my mind for a minute. Do you mind?"

The words she said hurt Jessica, but she knew she needed to give her some space. She could tell that if she pushed for more information or tried to tell Sarah how she felt about her, she would only shut down even more. "If that's what you want, I'll go work at the hotel."

"I'll drive you back over there." Sarah started to get up, but Jessica kept hold of her hand. Sarah sat back in the chair. She had no energy to fight her.

"I can make it back to the hotel on my own. Let me change and I'll give you some space. I...will you call me later tonight so I know you're home safely?"

"Yeah, I'll call. I'm going to go now. Will you lock the door?" She got up and set her cup in the sink. She moved around quickly as if she had to escape.

Jessica got up and moved toward her. She wrapped her arms around her, and she felt Sarah automatically return the hug, but she felt nothing. Jessica lowered her mouth to Sarah's and kissed her lightly and released her. Sarah went around her and grabbed the leash at the door and Benny was immediately beside her. And then they were gone.

Jessica rushed to the bedroom and brushed her teeth then pulled on the same clothes she had on the day before. She had to get out of this house. It felt terrible being here alone. She didn't make the bed or clean up her clothes. She raced through the house and checked the shop door. It was unlocked with all the lights on. She turned everything off and secured the door. She did the same with the back door. As she ran through the front room, she saw Sarah's phone on the stand by her recliner. She stopped. *She has no way to contact anyone if she needs help. God, I hope she knows where she's going and what she is doing.*

There was really nothing she could do about it at this point. Sarah drove off at least ten minutes earlier, and Jessica had no idea where she went. She shrugged and headed to the door again and then she turned around and picked up the phone. She scrolled through the directory. She found Patti and Patti Work at the top of the list of Ps. She pushed the button and a picture of Patricia showed on the screen. She held it to her ear.

"Why are you waking me on my day off? Why aren't you still making love to that gorgeous woman you brought to our house?" Patricia barked into the phone.

"Patricia, it's Jessica. She left, and I'm worried about her."

"Jessica, oh…what happened? What's going on?" Jessica could hear Patricia talking softly to Christine. "Go back to sleep, Christine." Jessica waited patiently.

"Where are you, Jessica? Tell me what happened."

"I'm about ready to leave Sarah's house. I told her this morning that I knew about Cheryl, and she froze up on me. I couldn't stand not telling her that I knew, but I pushed her away. She told me she needed some space, and she took Benny. She said she was going for a hike. She didn't take her phone, and she was so sad. I'm worried about her."

"This is my fault. I should've kept my mouth shut, but don't worry. She did this a lot for the first year or two after Cheryl was killed. She would disappear for an entire day. Christine and

I spent hours looking for her, and then late at night when we were ready to call the police, she would call us and tell us she was home. Finally, we just learned to let her be. She always came back to us. She'll be okay, trust me. Benny is with her, and Sarah's smart, the damn old G.I. How about you? Are you okay?"

"No, I don't think I am. I'm in love with her, and she made it clear to me this morning that what we were sharing was temporary, just for fun. I thought we both felt the same things. Now I'm afraid she won't let me close again, and I realize she never really let me in. I want to know her and love her. Is it a lost cause?"

"Jessica, honey, I don't like to think of anyone as a lost cause. She's bent but not broken. She needs you. She just doesn't know it. If you really care for her, you can't let one little setback like this end it. If you stick with her, there are going to be many more challenges before she'll really let you in, but I think she can. I do know she's worth it. She's scared of loving, of being disloyal to Cheryl, and scared of the pain that comes with losing someone you love. She's likely to push you away a few times before she learns that you are there to stay. If you run now, you'll never know what the two of you could have together. Give me a minute to get dressed, and I'll come pick you up. We'll get some breakfast and coffee, and I'll tell you about them and what happened. I've already pissed her off good, and you deserve to know."

Jessica sniffed through her quiet sobs. She wanted to talk to someone, and she wanted to know what Sarah had been through. "But it's your day off, and I need to work. Thank you, Patricia, but I'll be fine."

"You stay right there! I'll be over in fifteen minutes."

Jessica set the phone down and busied herself making the bed and picking up the bedroom and the bathroom. She washed the cups in the sink and the coffee pot. As she finished up, the bell rang. At the door, Patricia wrapped her arms around her. Jessica broke down and collapsed in her hug.

Patricia took Jessica to her favorite coffee shop. It was a small quiet place with only six tables decorated in art deco style. Jessica spent the morning hearing about what had happened to Cheryl over three years ago. With each word, Jessica hurt more and more for Sarah and the pain she suffered. By noon, Patricia dropped Jessica back at Sarah's house to get her car. They both hoped to see Sarah's truck in the drive when they pulled up, but they were disappointed to see the large empty space next to the side of the house. Jessica went to the front door and rang the bell. She didn't have a key, and she had locked up when Patricia came for her. She knew it was wishful thinking–no truck, no Sarah.

Jessica climbed into her big rental and drove back to the hotel. She managed just fine with only one wrong turn that brought her to the back of the hotel instead of the front, but she figured that out quickly enough. She had the valet park the car and went straight to her suite. She had convinced herself on the drive back that she would bury herself in work today. That was the defense mechanism she had used her whole life, and she had gotten behind on several of her accounts so there was plenty to do. When the elevator doors opened, the flowers Sarah had given her were still there, and she started to cry. The last thing she wanted to do was work. She poured a glass of wine and sat on the balcony, but after a few minutes, she found she couldn't sit still. *Is this what a broken heart feels like?* She set up her computer and began to go through e-mails with little success. After each e-mail she read, she got up from the desk and paced. Finally, she turned it into a routine—read an e-mail, walk around the suite, answer an e-mail, walk around the suite. Eventually, she managed to get through nearly all of the correspondence that had piled up over the last week or so. It was work she would have normally spent late nights working on, but her late nights had been occupied with something she had no idea she even wanted, let alone needed. Now she just hurt all over.

She managed to pass the time and noticed that it was getting dark. *Was Sarah still out on the trail?* She decided to try her cell. Maybe she had forgotten to call, but there was no answer. She sat back down at her computer contemplating what to do next. And the phone rang.

CHAPTER THIRTEEN

As soon as Sarah hit the trail, she knew she didn't want to be there. The sun on her face and the crisp fresh air felt good, but she missed Jessica, and it felt wrong to leave her with no explanation. She wanted to talk to her, but what would she say? She had kept a very important part of her life a secret from the woman she was falling in love with. She knew that was not the way to create a trusting relationship, but until she could resolve the constant struggle, she couldn't accept loving Jessica. She loved Cheryl and would always love Cheryl. She never dreamed she would ever even want to love someone again, let alone find someone who made her feel so good, so happy again.

Somehow, she managed to stroll slowly down one of her and Benny's favorite trails. Before she could see Jessica again, she had to come to terms with this. As she walked she knew she wanted to be with her, but could the rich, big city girl really find a place for the small-time woodworker who could barely make ends meet? In addition to all her baggage, there was millions of dollars and several hundred miles that separated them. She doubted that all these obstacles could be overcome.

Before she knew it, she was at the end of the five-mile hike. Thankfully, she had stopped at a convenience store and picked up water before she started. She realized the sun would be down before she made it back to the truck if she didn't hurry. Despite the awkward heavy work boots she was wearing because of her quick escape that morning, she started jogging back. While she jogged, she realized she really wanted to be with Jessica. Maybe if she took her own advice for once and talked through her concerns with Jessica, they could figure this all out.

At least she could find out what Jessica wanted in their relationship and maybe figure out a nice slow, easy path to follow. Given time to know each other—really know, with no more deep, dark secrets to hold back—then maybe they could get past what had seemed like impenetrable walls this morning. She wanted this. She wanted to live, and she wanted to share her life with Jessica, who for some reason, just appeared in her life. By the time she reached the truck, her feet were killing her. It was totally dark, but she felt better. She believed there was hope for her and Jessica. It wasn't going to be easy for her to open up, but if Jessica could just be patient with her, she knew they could figure it all out.

❖

Sarah saw her phone as soon as she entered and on it were several missed calls from Jessica. She realized she must be worried. Sarah felt badly for making her worry, especially after getting so upset at her when she had worried about Jessica. She pushed the button to return the missed call.

"Hello," Jessica answered timidly.

"Hi, Jess," Sarah said. "We're back home."

There was a long silence.

"Jessica, will you come by tomorrow? I guess we should talk. I need to work, though. I'm so far behind and the bills are piling up. Maybe like eight or so." She sounded more sober than she intended, but she was exhausted and needed to shower and get to bed. Tomorrow she would talk to Jessica, and they'd make a plan, or if Jess wanted no part of her, she would have to understand. She would just go back to her old routine. She knew how to do it—work, work, work. Her only concern now was, how much pain would losing Jessica cause if she didn't want a relationship?

"Okay. I'll see you then," Jessica said.

Sarah hung up and went through her evening routine and finally fell into her bed after she showered. After lying in the bed wishing for sleep most of the night, Sarah finally got up at six. It had been over a week since she had slept alone, and she missed having Jessica next to her. She hadn't even known how much she missed having someone in her life. She had worked so hard for so long to not feel, and she was finally feeling again. Even though it was scary, it was good. Despite all her worries from yesterday and her lack of sleep, Sarah actually felt better today. She was looking forward to seeing Jessica. She had missed being with her. There was still a lot to work out, but she believed it might be possible. Before she could give it too much thought, she made coffee and toast. She wanted to start building. Working in the shop always helped.

❖

Jessica got up early. She put on her running shoes and went down to the street. She hadn't run for a couple of weeks, and she knew it would help to get some good exercise. She was worried. She didn't want to lose Sarah. She knew she was in love, and for the first time, she understood what was missing in her life. She had always loved her work. She knew it would always be a very important part of her life, but she knew Sarah had turned something on inside her. It was something she would never be able to live without again. She also knew that Sarah was the only one who could fill that need.

Jessica started running with no real destination. Her only goal was to keep track of where she was. The last thing she needed was to get lost again. She quickly settled into an easy pace, and before she knew it, she had been running for nearly thirty minutes. She felt the pangs of hunger in her stomach, but just before she turned to go back to the hotel, she recognized Sarah's beautiful furniture in the window of the art shop as she ran past. They were the pieces Sarah had shown her on the plane, the ones for Meyer.

She stopped and stared; her work was amazing. An art studio was the right place for this furniture. Jessica wanted to buy all of the pieces. She could put it in the executive suites of her offices. Its modern clean lines fit perfectly with the style of her firm, and it had been several years since they had done something new in the offices. She and Mattie could take on the project, and they would have a blast working on it together. She had always hated the way it was decorated anyway. They had paid a decorator to come in a few years ago, and it just wasn't her style. She just didn't know what it needed and hadn't taken the time to work on it. Now she knew, and she would take the time. This was perfect, and it might allow Sarah the time and money to do some more design work. She looked at the window for open times and saw that the gallery would be open later today. Driven by the excitement of making the purchase, she cut almost five minutes off of her return trip to the hotel.

Jessica called for breakfast and jumped in the shower. At her desk with still wet hair and coffee cup in hand, the bell of the suite rang. She answered, "Yes?"

"Ma'am, there is a man here to see you. He says his name is Jimmy and that he's your driver. I was told your driver was out of town for the weekend and that you weren't to be disturbed. I'm sorry to bother you, but he insisted it was important to let you know he had returned." The desk receptionist sounded tired.

"Put him on the line."

"Good morning, ma'am." Jimmy's deep voice was comforting.

"Jimmy, what are you doing here? Why do I bother to tell you what to do? You never listen to me."

"Ma'am, Thanksgiving was very nice, but I told you I would be back today. Please call me if you need anything."

"Well, I'm not happy that you're back so early, but since you're here, can you take me to an art dealer at one o'clock today?"

"Yes, ma'am. Please give me the name, and I'll have the car ready at one," Jimmy answered quickly.

❖

The sun was setting fast when Sarah finally came back in the house. She hadn't finished as much as she had hoped, but she knew she could be ready to put on the first coat of finish before noon tomorrow. It was a good place to stop, and she wanted to have time to clean up before Jessica got there. As she headed to the bedroom, she picked up the phone and saw that there were six missed calls from David. It was odd that David would be so desperate to get in touch with her. She hoped that meant he had sold one of her pieces. It would help so much to get a little cash. Even with the sale of the hot tub and lathe, she was still going to be short this month. She had to get Joe the three thousand dollars she had promised, plus pay all the normal monthly bills. She had gotten so far behind, and her plan to squeeze in extra projects to make ends meet was failing dramatically.

Instead of listening to his voicemails, she hit the missed call button and connected with David.

"Sarah, did you hear my voicemail? Aren't you so excited? This is the craziest thing that has ever happened to me as a dealer. Can you believe it? I'm—"

"David, David—stop a minute. I didn't hear the voicemail. What's going on?"

"I sold every piece. This woman walked in today right after I opened and bought every one of your pieces. She actually paid me more than I was asking, insisting that she wanted to pay my commission, and she paid me in full today. I have an obscene amount of money here for you, girl. And I got a pretty large amount for myself, too. She insisted on paying my normal commission, not my special Sarah rate. How cool is that?" David finally stopped and took a big breath.

"David, what was the woman's name?" Sarah asked suspiciously.

"It was…let me look at the bill of sales…why do you care? Well, she was hot so…" he said. "I gave her your card. She's going to want more. She said something about decorating office suites in Chicago. Wait, here it is, Jessica Whitney. She was gorgeous—tall, dark hair, amazing body. What do you want me to do with your money?"

Sarah didn't say a word. She clicked off without responding to David.

CHAPTER FOURTEEN

Sarah had been sitting in her recliner staring out the window since she hung up with David. When the Lincoln rolled up to the front of her house, she ran out the door. She saw Jimmy jump out of the driver's door, and she stopped.

"Good evening, Ms. Sarah. How are you?"

Jessica climbed out of the backseat, stopped beside the car, and searched Sarah's face. "What's the matter?" she asked without a greeting.

"Jimmy, don't go anywhere." Sarah looked at Jimmy.

"Ma'am?" Jimmy asked looking at Jessica.

"Tell him to stay here!" Sarah's voice elevated.

"Jimmy, wait here for a minute."

"Please come in here now. I need to talk to you." Sarah again barked orders much like she did when she needed Airmen to do exactly what they were told with no questions.

Jessica followed her in the house. "What is wrong with you?"

"What is wrong with me? Who do you think you are? You think your money can just fix everything?" She was yelling now.

"Sarah...what? What is this all about?"

"You can't buy me, Jess. You can't fix this with money." She spread her arms out. "And I don't want your charity."

"Are you talking about the furniture I bought today?"

"What else? I want to buy it all back. I want you to take every penny back. I want you out of my life. I don't need your charity, and I don't want you to fix me."

"Sarah, please stop this. Can we just talk a minute? I bought the art because I think it's absolutely amazing work, and I want it in the offices back home. I've wanted it from the minute you showed it to me on the plane weeks ago."

"Bullshit."

"I'm not lying to you."

"I want you to leave." Sarah wouldn't make eye contact with her.

"Sarah, please. I didn't mean to offend you. I want the furniture. I bought it—"

"Leave! Now!" She opened the door.

Jessica looked at the door. She didn't want Jimmy to hear them. She looked at Sarah, but she still wouldn't look at her. She stood at the door, stiff and cold. She was still wearing her work clothes, and she looked exhausted. Jessica wanted to take her in her arms, but she could tell she would only push her away. She walked toward the door and paused a few inches from Sarah. She could feel the rage radiating from her. *How had this gotten so messed up?* She really did want the furniture. She had spent the afternoon creating new drawings of the offices with the pieces placed in just the right spots. She knew it would help Sarah financially, but she didn't believe that was the reason she bought the works, was it?

Jessica walked past Sarah fearing she would never see her again, but also feeling she had no choice. Jimmy was still standing outside of the car. He had to have heard most of the yelling. He opened the door for Jessica. She turned to look at Sarah's house before he drove away, but the door was already closed.

In the car, tears streamed down Jessica's face. She rarely cried. She had been taught it was a sign of weakness, and while she no longer thought of it as a weakness in others, she felt it was in her. For once, she wished she was in the limo so she could close the glass. She certainly didn't want Jimmy to see her cry.

"Ma'am, back to the hotel?" Jimmy tentatively asked.

She ducked her head down and wiped her eyes. "Yes, thank you." She was still running the whole situation over and over in her head. If she hadn't just found out that Sarah had lost her wife, she would never have let anyone talk to her like that, but the last thing she wanted to do was hurt Sarah, and somehow she had pushed her too far. She hated that it had ended this way, but mostly she hated that it had ended. Jessica knew as well as anyone how to climb into her work to avoid the feeling of hurt, but she was scared this time.

❖

Sarah got out of the shower almost as quickly as she had gotten in. She braided her hair, threw on some old pajama pants, and poured a drink. She had called Patricia as soon as Jimmy drove away. Sarah had sobbed telling the story, but she wasn't making much sense. Patricia finally insisted on driving over.

The bell rang and Patricia barged in without waiting for Sarah to come to the door. She yelled as she entered, "It's me, Benny. Don't kill me." Benny ran over and pushed into her leg with her nub spinning. Sarah was standing in the doorway of her bedroom. Patricia held a bag in her hand. "I brought you a sandwich, because I know you haven't eaten." She dropped the bag on the couch, marched directly to Sarah, and wrapped her arms around her.

Sarah couldn't have gotten away if she had tried, but she didn't try. She collapsed into Patricia's comforting strength. More than a few times, she had pulled her out of bed or off the floor curled next to Benny, after she had cried all night. Patricia was one of the only people she ever opened herself up to, mostly because Patricia forced her way into her heart.

"What is it, honey? What happened?"

"She bought all my furniture from David," Sarah said softly as she slumped onto the couch.

Patricia sat next to her with her hand on her shoulder. "Sarah, why is that so terrible?"

"Patti, can't you see? We're not right for each other, and it will only hurt more if I wait and find out later. She wants to fix me with money. Nothing will fix this." She put her hands over her heart. "I'll always love Cheryl, and I'll always miss her. She was my...my life."

Patricia looked at her hard. "Who are you trying to convince? Yourself? Because you're afraid to love again?" Patricia brushed the back of her hand across Sarah's cheek. "What makes you think she wants you to forget Cheryl or stop loving her?"

"She's a rich girl, and she's always had it her way. I can't be bought." Sarah raised her voice again. Maybe her irrational thoughts would sound better if she said it louder.

"Honey, I don't think she was trying to buy you."

"It's just not right, and I'm not ready. It shouldn't be this hard, should it?" Sarah looked at her and wiped her eyes and nose with the back of her hand.

Patricia grabbed the Kleenex box off the sofa table and handed it to Sarah. "You know anything worth having is hard. It's always complicated. I know she cares about you very much. You should call her."

"I can't. It's best if we stop now before we're in so deep we really hurt each other. I can't live in her world, and I don't think I can let her in mine. Can you imagine me with her wealthy friends?"

"It sounds like you're pretty worried about her money. That doesn't sound like something you would care about." Patricia looked at Sarah. "Has she ever said anything about money?"

"No. What would she say? 'So, Sarah, this lack of money issue you have, you better fix that or we can't go out'?" Sarah said sarcastically.

"Seriously, you know she's not like that."

"Besides, I can't call her. I kicked her out of my house and embarrassed both of us in front of her driver. It truly is better. We can just go back to our lives."

"Because you really liked it so much the way it was? Working yourself to the bone and having dinner once a week with your two old women friends? Sarah, you love her, and she loves you. It's okay to love again. You can work this out. I know she'll let you take time to figure out how to open up to love again. Don't let this go."

Sarah didn't say anything. She just sat looking back at her, and the tears began to roll down her face again. Patricia wrapped her big soft arms around her. "I know it hurts, honey. I'm so sorry."

After a few minutes, Patricia walked Sarah to her bed and pulled off her old tennis shoes. She tugged the comforter over her and left her to sleep. Sarah could hear Patricia on the phone. "Chris, she's not doing well. I'm going to sleep on the couch. I'll be home in the morning." After a pause, Patricia spoke again. "I'll tell you in the morning. I love you."

When Sarah headed out to her shop in the morning, she left Patricia asleep on the couch. Sarah was putting a coat of lacquer on the dresser. It would be ready to deliver tomorrow. By noon tomorrow, she could turn it into some much needed cash.

Patricia made her way out to the shop when she finally got up. "I'll put the coffee on."

"Okay. Give me a minute to finish up, and I'll be in," Sarah said almost too cheerfully.

Soon enough, Sarah popped in, just as Patricia sat down at the table to wait for her. "You didn't need to stay. You weren't worried I'd off myself, were you?" Sarah laughed.

"Sarah, that's not funny. I was worried about you. No, I didn't think you were going to hurt yourself, but I was worried," Patricia said. "You seem better."

"I was thinking about what you said, and maybe I should call her. The lacquer dries fast so I was thinking I'd get a couple more coats on the dresser, and then I'd call her and see if she wanted to have a late lunch." Sarah pulled two cups out of the cabinet and started pouring coffee before it was done brewing. "Do you think she'll talk to me?"

"I'm a bit confused, but I do think it's a good idea to talk to her. It sounds like you still don't know what you want for sure. One minute you're pushing her away, and the next minute you're running to her. I think you need to really think about this so you don't mess with her anymore."

"I know you're right. This is hard for me. I never thought I would ever feel anything for anyone ever again, and I've fallen in love. I couldn't handle losing someone again. It would kill me. I worked so hard to be able to function again so I'm still struggling, even if I do know I love her. She's truly amazing, smart, and so together. We can talk so easily, and it's so nice to just be with her. It feels so good."

Patricia smiled at her. "It is obvious how you feel about her. It was obvious from the minute I saw you together. Just make sure you can do this without pushing her away again. If you pull her back to you, and then you push her away again, there probably won't be a third chance for this. She has some vulnerability too, you know?"

"I know you're right." Sarah sipped her coffee processing Patricia's words and remembering how fragile Jessica had seemed when she told her about her family.

"Honey, I have to get home and shower and get over to my office. Call me later if you need to talk about this. Just be careful with both of your hearts."

❖

Jessica got up early. Her head was filled with thoughts of Sarah, but she wanted to get to work and stop dwelling on something she couldn't change. She showered quickly and was dressed, reading her e-mail when Jimmy called. She met him downstairs.

"Good morning, ma'am."

"Hi, Jimmy," she said as he held the door for her.

He hurried to the driver's side and climbed in. "Are you still planning to go to the job site first thing?"

"Yes. They should be waiting for us."

They drove in silence to the building location. Jimmy pulled the car up next to the construction trucks. "Wow, I didn't know so much of it was already done," Jimmy said.

"Yeah, much of the steel structure was started earlier in the year and halted briefly this fall for some changes and then they opted for a new architect. That's when I rolled in."

The foreman met her at the car with an extra hardhat in his hand. "Good morning, ma'am. I'm Ramon Martinez, the site foreman. Mr. Wilson asked me to show you whatever you wanted to see." He extended a hand and then gave her the hardhat.

"Thank you, Ramon. I just need to see the changes to the design on the main level. I hear that has caused a lot of additional work. I want to see how it's progressing." Really, she wanted to make sure they made the changes she wanted. Rodney had made no secret at his frustration about making such major changes to the structure.

"We're just finishing up. It provided us with a few challenges, but nothing we couldn't handle." He laughed. "It's coming together nicely though. I think you'll be pleased. Follow me." He walked ahead of her.

Jessica followed, putting on her hardhat. "Have you been the foreman from the beginning of construction?"

"Yes, ma'am. I was on at the beginning and came back when they resumed construction." He walked quickly around equipment and construction materials.

Jessica did acrobatic maneuvers to navigate with her heels on. She knew she shouldn't have worn her heels out here, but she didn't want to have to change for morning meetings. Besides, she had learned to manage quite well on any job site.

"Here you go, ma'am." Ramon pointed out the changes they had completed to meet the new design.

"This looks great, Ramon. Your team is doing good work."

"Thank you, ma'am. What else can I show you?"

"Is the rest of the work on schedule?" she asked him directly. He apparently wasn't trying to hide anything from her, and she really didn't want to traipse around the site all morning.

"Yes, ma'am. We'll be back on schedule by the end of the month," he said confidently.

"Great. Then I'm done here." She turned back in the direction of the car. Jessica had seen enough from the short tour. She felt they had adequately made the changes, and the delay wouldn't have too much impact on the cost.

Ramon walked behind her and held out his hand when they reached the car. "Let me know if you want to see anything else."

She shook his hand and took off the hardhat, returning it to him. "I'll stop by periodically when I'm in town. Thank you, Ramon."

"Anytime."

Jimmy was already holding the door open for her. "Okay, ma'am. Where would you like to go?"

"Back to the contractor's office, but let's stop to pick up a sandwich at the deli on the way so I have something to eat while I wait."

"The one by the hotel or the one by the contractor's offices?"

"I prefer the one next to the contractor's office," she said while staring at messages on her phone. There were three messages from Mattie about another project in Chicago. It looked like there were some problems. She'd call when she got to Wilson's office. It was easier to do when she had her computer and could make notes.

Jimmy ran in and got the sandwiches and dropped her off in front of the large building before noon. She got in the elevator and as she stood there alone, her thoughts wandered back to her evening with Sarah. As long as she was busy she could let it go, but the minute she slowed down, it washed over her like a heavy wave.

When the elevator door opened, she was greeted by Mr. Wilson's secretary. "Good morning, Ms. Whitney. You're here early. The meetings don't start until three."

"I was hoping there would be some place I could sit and have a sandwich. I need to call my office and do some other work." She held up her computer.

"Yes, ma'am. Back here is an empty office. I escape back here and close the door when I need a break sometimes. The computer is on the network and the phone is right there. Just push nine for an outside line."

"This is perfect. Thank you so much."

"Of course. Is there anything else you need?"

Jessica shook her head and settled into the big chair. She punched in Mattie's number right away, leaving herself no more time to think.

Jessica talked with Mattie and spent the next three hours handling a difficult client. She was the diplomat and handled these challenging issues better than her partners, but she was pushed to her absolute limit when Wilson's secretary knocked on the door to remind her that her meeting with Wilson's staff was about to begin.

Jessica was beginning to think the day was never going to end. It was getting late, and she was sitting in yet another meeting. She had managed to get her mind off Sarah when she was really busy, but she was struggling now to think of anything but Sarah. Besides, she felt a little like they were just trying to kiss her ass. She had gotten pretty frustrated with them earlier over some costs to the construction changes, and she made sure they knew she could walk away with no major impact on her firm if they didn't stop jerking her around. Now for the third time today, they were explaining how they would make the changes and were even offering to suck up the extra cost. She knew threatening to leave them was a risk to the success in the region, but she had no patience for any more delays, especially today. She normally made herself and her standards clear upfront, but she was having such a good time with Sarah perhaps she had lost her edge, or was she just being edgy now?

Jessica stood. She couldn't take it anymore. "Gentlemen, I've heard enough. You're repeating yourselves, and I'm too busy to sit through this again."

She packed up her laptop and briefcase while they watched her—somewhat stunned. "I'm heading back to Chicago at the end of the week. I want updates twice a week including images from the site. Don't insult me by sending photos that don't show the critical areas. I'll be working with the buyer most of the rest of the week." She walked out.

When she reached the lobby, Jimmy wasn't there. She reached in her briefcase for her cell phone. It wasn't there. She knew immediately that she had left it in the car.

It was later than she thought. The sun had set hours ago. The building's exterior bulbs provided the only light and the reception area was closed. She knew the hotel wasn't too far, but she really didn't want to walk that far in heels. Jimmy was likely nearby, and if she waited in the lobby he would be around soon. The effect of walking out of a meeting in frustration would be greatly diminished if she was sitting in the lobby waiting for her driver when the other members of the meeting left the building. They would want to offer her a ride and that would be lame, so she pulled her coat on and began to walk.

Jessica hurt inside from the pure feeling of loss. There was a hole, like someone took a piece of her away. She hadn't known it could be filled, but now it seemed rawer for having been satisfied briefly, only for the gift to be yanked from her. She wanted to go to Sarah and tell her she understood what she had done wrong, but she was afraid she would throw her out again. Her pride couldn't take that and her heart would probably explode. Small tears formed in her eyes, but she refused to cry anymore.

The chill in the air made her quicken her pace, but it didn't stop her from thinking of all the memories they had shared in the short time they had known each other. She missed Sarah. She wanted her back, but she was mad at herself for wanting something she couldn't have.

She had spent her life getting what she wanted. If you could work hard to get it, she would succeed. She didn't fool around with things she couldn't work hard to get. She had always felt it wasn't realistic to dream of those things, and it was a waste of time. The loss of her mother and later her father had taught her that. Now she found herself dreaming of something she was sure was gone, and she was still confused about how she had lost it.

After she had been walking for too long, she realized she was not where she was supposed to be. It was dark, and there were only a few streetlights very far apart creating long, eerie shadows. There was an overpass in front of her. She could hear the traffic above her. The walls of the buildings around her were covered in green, red, and yellow symbols painted on top of each other in a collage of indecipherable images. When she heard muffled voices around the corner, she turned to retrace her steps and increased her pace. Finally, she pulled off her heels and started to jog.

"Hey. Hey, lady, come back here!" She heard one of the husky voices from behind her.

Jessica felt her heart rate increase as she breathed in and out quickly. She dropped her shoes and began to move faster, the tingly feeling of adrenaline carrying her.

Jessica heard running from behind her. She dropped her computer and briefcase and sped up. Her skirt bunched up around her thighs, and she ran faster. Her bare feet burned with scrapes and cuts from the rocks and hard concrete.

She made it about a hundred yards before one of the men grabbed her from behind and another rushed in front of her. "Hey, dude. She dropped a computer. Looks like a real nice one. We can get something for that and maybe there's some money in this briefcase. Let the bitch go," she heard a kid's voice from behind her.

"Let me go. Just let me go. Take the stuff," Jessica said calmly, attempting to sound strong.

"Why? You look like a rich bitch, and you were stupid enough to come into my territory. You're a fucking fool, and now you're mine." The short, stocky man in front of her looked at her with squinted eyes and a clenched jaw. She saw a hate in those eyes that had been brewing for years. A much bigger man held her from behind.

She knew this wasn't going to end well so she began to struggle and felt the man's grip tighten on her wrists. She managed to get one hand away and spun around. She landed one good punch to his groin. He doubled over in pain just long enough for her to slip out of his grip, but she felt her shoulder pop as she pulled away. The pain she felt was so intense it ran through her whole arm like a knife blade. Jessica screamed and ran hard while yelling for help. She made it a few more feet before she was dropped to the ground. The first blow to her head came immediately. She thought for sure her eye was going to explode. She didn't feel the second or any of the many that followed it.

CHAPTER FIFTEEN

Sarah was sitting in her recliner dressed in gray slacks and a burgundy blouse. She had dozed off. After two nights of no sleep, she was exhausted. She had finished putting lacquer on the dresser as she had hoped and then showered and started calling Jessica around three o'clock. She left a nice simple voicemail the first time. "Jess, please call me back. I'm sorry, and I want to talk to you." She was sure Jessica would call her as soon as she heard it. Jessica was probably mad, but she was a rational woman. She would at least hear her out. She didn't worry. Sarah knew how serious Jessica's work was, and she was probably in a meeting. She would call when she got the message.

Sarah had busied herself working at her computer. She updated some advertising on her website. She made some calls and arranged for two more projects. Then she tried twice more to reach Jessica and decided to settle into her recliner for a minute. If she didn't hear from her soon, she would go to the hotel and beg her forgiveness. She'd solicit Jimmy to help her if she needed to. In the meantime, she was going to assume Jessica was working late and just rest a minute.

The buzzing of her phone woke her up. It was dark out, but she had no idea what time it was or how long she had been sleeping. She picked up the phone without looking. She was going to fix this. "Hello. Thank you for calling me back. I'm sor—"

"Ma'am?" a deep masculine voice said.

"Who is this?" Sarah was surprised.

"Ma'am, my name is Justin Downing. I'm a police officer. I'm at the hospital. We just brought in a young lady tonight. She had no identification, but she had a business card in her coat. Are you Sarah Jarrett?"

"Yes." Sarah's head spun. This didn't make sense. "Is she okay? What happened? I'll be there in a few minutes. Which hospital?" Sarah didn't want to believe it could be Jessica. Her heart sank, and she felt weak. She didn't know if she could do this.

"She's at St. Luke's Medical Center. Do you think you can help identify her?" the officer asked.

"I'm afraid it might be Jessica Whitney." She knew it was her. The realization got her moving. "Is she okay?"

"Ma'am, are you next of kin?"

"*Is she okay?*" She yelled in the phone as she rushed to get her shoes on.

"Ma'am, I can't answer—"

Sarah clicked off her phone and ran to her truck.

She drove too fast in the direction of St. Luke's. Sarah was driven by pure panic. A metallic taste filled her mouth as the adrenaline pumped through her. She felt shaky, but focused on getting to the hospital as quickly as she could. Traffic was relatively light this time of night, but every driver on the road seemed to be crawling and in her way. She hadn't been in St. Luke's in over three years. She was scared to death. She couldn't do this again. How could this happen? She had worked so hard to protect herself from this pain, and she was facing it again.

Sarah couldn't help but fear the worst. She had been thinking all day of fixing things with Jessica and making a plan to build a real relationship with her.

Sarah parked haphazardly in the emergency room parking area and ran to the door. A rush of anxiety flooded through her as bright white fluorescent lights and the sterile hospital smell hit her. She slowed down to look around the waiting area trying to get her bearings. The place was nearly empty. There was a woman and child sitting in the corner, but there was no one else in sight. Sarah spun around desperate for someone to help her find Jessica. She spotted the reception desk. There was a young woman sitting at a computer. "I'm looking for Jessica Whitney. She was brought here tonight with some kind of injury."

The woman looked up from the computer and paused for a minute as if thinking about what she just heard. "You must be talking about our Jane Doe, brought in this evening badly beaten. She's still unconscious. I think there's a detective somewhere around here."

"Beaten?" Sarah hadn't even stopped to think about why she might be here. "Beaten?" she repeated. "What happened to her? I need to see her."

"Ma'am, let's find the detective." The woman got up from behind the desk and motioned for Sarah to follow her. "There's a lounge down here where the cops hide out."

Sarah's heart was racing. She was frustrated at being dragged around the hospital. All she wanted to do was find Jessica, to hold her and beg her forgiveness, and know that she was going to be okay. She didn't see any alternative, so she followed the woman.

She pushed open a door to reveal a small lounge with two round tables, a half dozen chairs, and a sofa. The room was occupied by one man. It had been several years, but she recognized him from Cheryl's office functions. Sarah was a bit taken aback by seeing someone from Cheryl's past.

He looked up from the papers in front of him when he saw her. He stood up. "Ms. Jarrett…Sarah. How are you?"

"Tim?"

"Yes, Tim Connors. I'm glad you remember. When Officer Downing called this in and I heard your name in association with the victim, I volunteered to take this case."

"Where's Jessica, and how is she?" she blurted out, making no effort to conceal her concern and impatience.

"Sarah, please sit down. I'll tell you as much as I can. I know you must be worried, so first, the doctor believes she'll recover completely. She is still unconscious right now, and she is in serious condition. She's in the ICU, and I don't think they will let anyone but family in to see her." He hurried through those details hoping to calm her a bit so he could get some information.

"She has no family here. She's from Chicago, and I have no idea how to contact her family. Please let me see her."

"You know I have nothing to do with that, but I do know the doc. I'll talk to her and see what I can do. If you will please just tell me as much as you can first." Tim looked seriously at her.

"I know her name and…wait, she has a chauffeur. He came with her on this trip. Jimmy, where was he?" Sarah stopped. "That's it. That's really all I know." Tears formed in the corners of her eyes. Sarah was so frustrated, she stood and paced around the chair only to sit right back down. She just wanted to be with Jessica.

"Sarah, it's okay." Tim touched her hand. "Do you know where she was staying? Maybe we can find her driver there."

"Of course. He'll be there. I'll go get him." She jumped to her feet and would have been to her truck in a minute if Tim hadn't grabbed her arm.

"No, wait. I'll send a uniform to pick him up. You need to stay here. If she wakes up and asks for you, we want someone she knows to comfort her. Where is she staying?"

"Oh yeah…yeah…the Ritz. She has the Presidential Suite at the Ritz."

"Okay. You stay here. I'll call and get someone over there."

Before he could walk out, Sarah's phone rang. She didn't recognize the number and normally wouldn't have answered it, but she answered just to make the annoying ring stop. "Hello."

"Ms. Sarah, it's Jimmy. I'm sorry to bother you, but I can't find Ms. Whitney. She left the—"

"Jimmy, where are you? She's at the hospital. Jimmy, it's bad. I need—"

"Where? Where is she? Give me the address."

His voice was shaky. Sarah could tell he was running. "She's at St Luke's." She didn't know the address. She just knew where it was, but before she could say another word, Jimmy had clicked off and she stood silently, stunned.

"Sarah? Was that the chauffeur?" Tim asked. Sarah swayed a bit, and he rushed to catch her. He sat her on the sofa. "Are you okay? I'll get the nurse."

Sarah breathed in deeply and then shook her head. "I'm okay. Jimmy's on his way. He'll know something," she said as she stared blankly across the room.

"I'm so sorry. It must be hard for you to be here. Let me get you some water."

"No, tell me what happened."

"It's pretty bad. I don't—" He avoided eye contact with her.

"Tell me." Sarah looked directly at him.

He squirmed and took her hands in his before he started. "Two uniforms were on patrol in Alhambra District near Bethany Home Road."

"What was she doing in Alhambra?"

"I'm not sure. It doesn't make sense. The uniforms, they drove right up on the guys. They caught one of the men, but two others got away. She was unconscious when they arrived on scene. The ambulance brought her here. When the uniforms called in, I took the call. I'm Mark's partner now. He's on another case or he would've come too."

"Was she raped?" Sarah had slipped back into a zone.

"No, Sarah. She wasn't raped. She was badly beaten though, and if the uniforms hadn't arrived when they did, those idiots would have killed her. She's pretty bruised—lots of lacerations on her face and her knees and legs. Doc says her shoulder was dislocated. It appears she put up one helluva fight." He looked at Sarah. She was still staring off into space, but when he stopped, she looked over at him. He went on. "The worst is the head injuries. Doc says it looks like they may have banged her head on the concrete. Her face is pretty cut up. She was their punching bag."

Sarah turned away again. "Please, Tim. Get me in to see her."

"I'll see what I can do. We need to get in contact with her family." She knew he was putting her off. All she could do now was wait for Jimmy. He would know something. They sat in silence.

Finally, Sarah could no longer stand the silence. "Why isn't he here yet?"

Then, as if on cue, Jimmy swung the door open and it slammed into the wall with a thud. Sarah and Tim both jumped to their feet.

Sarah crossed the room, and they embraced. Jimmy held her shoulders and backed her away so he could see her face. "Is she okay? She left without me. This is my fault, Sarah." His eyes filled with tears.

Sarah squeezed his hand. "Jimmy, this is Tim. He's a detective and needs to get information from you. Please tell him everything." Tim stuck out his hand and Jimmy took it. He motioned him to a table.

Jimmy gave Tim all the phone numbers he had and told the story of the entire day. "Here's her phone. It may have numbers on it you can use." Jimmy handed her iPhone over to him. "I found her phone when I realized she had left before I returned from getting a sandwich. I think I must have only missed her by a few minutes, but I didn't realize she was gone until I saw all the men she was meeting with leave the building. So I went out to the car and called her while I was considering where to look for her. Her phone rang in the back seat. I drove back to the hotel, and when she wasn't there I retraced every route I knew from the offices to the hotel. I was so worried. I knew something went wrong. It's out of character for her to leave without telling me where she is going." He stopped for a minute. "I finally decided to call Ms. Sarah to see if she knew where she was just so I would know she was safe."

❖

Sarah paced back and forth across the waiting room floor. They'd been waiting for over an hour and there was no sign of Tim. She knew he was busy trying to contact Jessica's family, but she was going crazy. She needed to see her. Sarah smacked her palms against the wall and rested her forehead against the cold cinder blocks. She was crawling out of her skin.

Jimmy had been watching her. He walked over to where she stood. He hesitated a minute, and then touched her shoulder gently. "Ms. Sarah." She turned and looked up at him with tears in her eyes. "I'm going to hold you tight." He held out his arms, and she fell into him. His strong arms pulled her close to him. "We'll get it all figured out. She's going to be fine. We have to believe that." He leaned his cheek on the top of her head. "Please don't cry." He moved her toward the chairs and lowered her into one of them.

"Jimmy, thank you. Thank you for being here. Do you know any of her family?"

"I saw her dad one time when she met him for lunch. I didn't actually meet him. That's not exactly my place, but normally, Ms. Whitney introduces me to people who ride with us. I took him back to his office. They didn't speak during the ride, and I could've cut the tension in the car with a knife. I was glad when he got out. I never ask her about anything, but she trusts me and sometimes tells me things. All she said that day was that she would never talk to him again. As far as I know, she hasn't and that was maybe three or four years ago."

"Is there anyone else? Aunt or cousin?" Sarah asked.

"I'm sorry, ma'am. I don't think so. She's never spoken of anyone except her grandfather who passed when she was still in college."

"What are we going to do? How are we going to get in to see her?" Sarah thought out loud. "Wait! My best friend is a lawyer. Maybe she can tell me if there is anything we can do." Sarah looked at Jimmy's Timex–almost eleven. They would be asleep, but she punched the button on her phone with Christine's face on it. As it was ringing, Tim returned to the waiting room. She clicked off after only one ring to hear what he had to say.

"Jimmy, Mr. Jarrett is on the line, and he wants to talk to you. Please come with me."

Sarah's phone rang. Christine was calling back. "Chris, I need your help." Her voice sounded panicked in her own head.

"Sarah, where are you?" Christine's voice was groggy from sleep.

Sarah explained everything as quickly as she could. Christine said she would start looking into it to see what she could do, but as long as there was a next-of-kin, there was likely nothing to be done. "Here, talk to Patricia. I'll call one of my colleagues."

"Hi, honey. What's going on?" Patti asked.

Sarah retold the story and stopped abruptly as Jimmy walked in the room. "Patti, I have to go."

Jimmy's dark skin had turned to an ashy gray.

"What is it?" Sarah asked.

"He said he wouldn't be here until the weekend. He was too busy and felt there was nothing he could do anyway."

"Are you kidding? She's in critical condition, and he's not coming out?"

"No, ma'am. He said if he had time he would come out on Saturday, but that he had arranged with the doctors to have her flown back to Chicago as soon as she was stable. He told me to stay with her and take care of her business here." Jimmy stopped and stared at her for a minute. "Ms. Sarah, I don't know what to do. I can find my way around any city, and I can protect her from the physical threats when she doesn't leave me behind, but I don't know the first thing about...I don't know what to do."

"Jimmy, will they let you see her? Did he give you permission to go see her?"

"What?" He looked at her, appearing to slowly take in what she had said. "Yeah, I told them you should go be with her."

"Okay…uhh…" She paced around him a bit processing what was happening. "It's up to us to take care of her, Jimmy. We love her. We can help her." She said it, but didn't know for sure what to do.

"You should go in her room and be with her. They said only one of us at a time."

"Yeah, we'll figure out what to do in the morning." Sarah walked toward the ICU.

Jimmy seemed to be getting his thoughts together. "Don't worry about that. I'll call Mr. Stewart, her partner at the firm. He'll take care of the rest."

❖

The doctor at the ICU desk was waiting for her. "Ms. Jarrett, I'm Dr. Barbara Lue. I'm the neurosurgeon. I was on call when Ms. Whitney was admitted. I'm so sorry about your friend."

"Thank you. May I see her now?" Sarah's patience had been worn to a thread.

"Yes, of course. Let me explain her condition and what you're going to see. It can be a little shocking." She looked at Sarah seriously. "Ms. Whitney is in a coma due to the brain trauma she experienced, and that in turn has caused a cerebral edema, and—"

"Excuse me, Doctor. I don't know what that means." Sarah was already frustrated with this exchange of medical terms.

"I'm sorry. A cerebral edema is a large accumulation of fluid around the brain. It's generally caused by some type of injury to the brain. In Ms. Whitney's case, it was from blows to the back of her head."

Sarah winced.

"Her CT shows a skull fracture that may be causing additional pressure on her brain and some bleeding."

"Oh my God! That sounds so bad." She thought for a minute and asked. "Is she going to be all right?"

"I'm afraid it's pretty bad. She may require surgery if the pressure has an effect on the amount of blood supply getting to her brain or if it blocks the flow of spinal fluid. We have inserted a device in her cranium to monitor the pressure inside her skull. With this device in place, we'll know immediately if there are changes in her condition, and then we can operate right away to reduce the pressure. We really don't want to operate unless it's absolutely necessary. We have her on some medication that should help control the inflammation."

"Will that help bring her out of the coma?" Sarah was overwhelmed by all the information. "I just want her to be okay."

"We hope so. Comas are hard to predict, but actually, as long as there is swelling, a coma isn't necessarily a bad thing. However, even when the swelling goes down, she could remain in a coma. She's still in critical condition, but she's stable now. There's a good chance she'll come through this with no long term affects."

Dr. Lue took Sarah's arm and began to lead her to a small room in the far corner of the mostly empty ICU. "Just so you aren't shocked by her appearance, she was badly beaten, and she's on a respirator. We may be able to remove that in the morning if she is progressing well. We'll discuss it with Mr. Price. Some prefer the breathing be regulated when the patient is in a coma, but I don't like to leave anyone on a respirator unless it is absolutely necessary."

"Mr. Price. Do you mean Jimmy? He's responsible for her care?" Sarah asked.

"Yes. Her father already sent the power of attorney."

"Poor Jimmy."

"Yes, he seems a little overwhelmed. I'm sure he would appreciate your counsel."

They entered Jessica's room. She felt a heavy pressure in her chest as she walked into the cold gray room. As she got closer, the tears streamed down her cheeks. Jessica's face was badly bruised and cut up. There was a crescent-shaped gash above her left eye. The ventilator tube was taped to the side of her mouth, distorting her features even more. The methodical sound of the machines took her back to the horrifying night of Cheryl's death. She shook her head in an attempt to erase the image. Jessica's right arm was immobilized in a sling, and she could see bruising around her collarbone at the top of the hospital gown. Sarah moved to the opposite side of the bed and lightly took Jessica's hand in both of hers.

"Jessica, my poor girl. I'm so sorry. I love you. I need you. Please get better. Please hear me." She leaned her head on Jessica's forearm. "I'm here, baby. I'm here. Jimmy's here, too. We both love you. We're going to take care of you. Oh, Jess, I'm so sorry. I was so mean to you."

Sarah sat holding Jessica's hand all night long.

CHAPTER SIXTEEN

I didn't know you knew each other." Sarah yelled so the two women could hear her. They were laughing and talking to each other as they crossed the street. The sun was bright orange shining in her eyes but she recognized them both.

"We're friends," Jessica yelled back.

Sarah stood in front of the diner staring at the two beautiful women waiting for them to get to her.

"Watch out!" Sarah ran toward them when she saw the tall man in a red baseball cap reach for a gun. The sound of the two shots rang out with a loud crack. She screamed as Cheryl and Jessica hit the black pavement; one on each side of the bright white lines.

"Cheryl, Jess—" Sarah jerked and looked up at the nurse standing over her.

"You were calling out in your sleep. Bad dream?"

"Ah...yeah. I just—" She looked over at Jessica lying motionless in the bed. "Has there been any change?"

"No. No change. But there's a big man at the desk asking to see you. He said his name is Jimmy."

"Can you tell him I don't want to leave her alone?" Her voice was dry and scratchy.

"He is pretty intimidating, ma'am, and he was adamant about seeing you."

"Jess, baby. I love you. Please hear me. I'll be right back. I promise." Sarah stood on creaky, stiff legs and walked to the desk.

Jimmy was still wearing the same suit he had on when he came in last night, and his face was covered with a thick black stubble. Sarah knew he probably hadn't even left the hospital.

He met her and pulled her into his arms. "Oh, Ms. Sarah, you look exhausted."

"I'm okay." She tried to stand taller. "I need to get back in there to be with her. If she wakes up, I don't want her to be alone." She pushed gently out of his embrace. She was focused and functioning on adrenaline.

"You need to go home. Go take a shower and get a nap. I'll stay here with her until you get back." Jimmy wasn't leaving much room for discussion.

"Jimmy, you haven't slept either. Maybe I can doze off a bit. I can't leave. I just can't." She was afraid to sleep—the dreams were too real and too terrible.

"You won't listen to me, will you?"

Sarah shook her head.

"Okay. You go back in, but I'm going to go get you something to eat. I'm going to go shower, and I'll be back in forty minutes tops."

She grabbed his big hand and smiled. "Thank you."

Sarah headed back to the ICU, and she thought of Benny. "Jimmy, wait!" He had started for the elevator.

"Can you go in with her for a few minutes? I have to call my friend to take care of Benny. She's been in the house all night. I'll only be a minute." She saw the discomfort in his face.

"Okay."

She touched his arm as he walked past, in an effort to comfort him. "Do you have the phones?"

He turned and handed her three cell phones, hers, his, and Jessica's.

Sarah took the elevator to the ground floor and went outside. The fresh air felt good. The sun was just coming up and there was still the morning chill in the air. She opened her phone and pushed the picture of Patricia.

"Hello, honey. How is she? And how are you?" Patricia didn't even give Sarah a chance to greet her.

"Patti, I'm so scared." Sarah wept into the phone. She continued through loud sobs in an effort to catch her breath. "She was beaten badly, and she's in a coma."

"Oh, sweetie. I'm so sorry. What can I do? You want me to come to the hospital? I can take off today."

"I just need you to go get Benny. Can she stay with you for a couple of days? I'll have the kennel pick her up."

"Christine picked her up last night. She is not going to the kennel. She can stay here as long as you need her to. She's a little confused, but content. What else do you need?"

"You guys are so good to me. Thank you and thank Chris for me." Sarah felt a rush of gratitude, and tears began to fall again. Chris and Patti had always been there for her even when she was barely among the living.

"Sarah, we'll help however we can."

"Could you bring me some clean clothes—just some jeans and a couple of T-shirts and underclothes? Oh, and a toothbrush. I can probably find a shower in the hospital somewhere."

"Of course. I'll be over in an hour or so."

"Thank you." Sarah clicked off and headed back to the elevator. She really was exhausted, but she didn't want to fall asleep.

❖

"You should talk to her. They say it helps if you try to reach her—maybe some things you've done together." The nurse entered the room for regular rounds.

"I'm afraid I couldn't talk too long. I've only really known her a few weeks. They have been the most amazing and wonderful weeks, but…"

"You could read to her. Do you know what kind of books she likes?"

"That's a great idea. When you go back out would you tell Jimmy to pick up a copy of *Pride and Prejudice* for me to read to her?"

"Of course. That's an excellent choice. He'll be glad for something to do. Poor man."

Sarah watched through the glass as the nurse relayed to Jimmy her request. She saw the smile form on his face. He looked over at her through the glass to Jessica's room, gave a thumbs up, and then he disappeared.

Sarah quickly realized her twenty-four-hour vigil was impossible and managed to sleep a little out of pure exhaustion. The nursing staff had been kind to her and Jimmy. They let him sleep on the couch in the lounge where he was able to doze off for a few hours, and they brought Sarah pillows and a blanket. She managed a few hours curled up on two leather lounge chairs pushed together next to Jessica's bed.

It was nearly noon, and Sarah was starting chapter seventeen. *"Elizabeth related to Jane, the next day, what had passed…."* Sarah stopped and looked up as Dr. Lue entered.

"Good morning, Sarah. Have you slept at all?"

"I managed to get a few hours last night."

"I know it will do no good to tell you to go get some real rest so I won't bother." Dr. Lue pulled Jessica's chart.

"Is there any change, Doctor?" Sarah asked eagerly. "The nurses won't tell me anything."

"I'm afraid the nurses don't want to tell you what you don't want to hear. Seems you and Jimmy have endeared yourself to a pretty tough staff," she said and then her tone turned somber. "I'm sorry. There's no change, Sarah. We're going to make some adjustments to her medications this afternoon. I know this must be discouraging for you, but I'm still hopeful. She had a very bad injury, and her reaction is not unusual." She went to Sarah and took her hand. "This is good what you are doing. It really is helpful for her to hear your voice."

Sarah nodded.

"I'll be back with Dr. Brennan first thing tomorrow with the new prescription for the nurses to adjust."

Sarah pulled her two chairs together to get some sleep. She was exhausted.

"Good night, Sarah. Try to sleep. I could get you a mild sleeping pill. Dr. Martin in the ER, would surely give you something. He's a good guy."

"No. I want to be able to wake up if she needs me." Sarah lay down in a little ball and surprisingly sleep came.

It was too bright. Sarah walked toward the door wondering why it was so bright. The ICU was normally dimly lit. At the door, she saw Benny, lying on the floor waiting just outside Jessica's room. She was holding her nighttime vigil here in the hospital. "Benny, you can't be here. Did Patti bring you up here? She's going to get us all in trouble." Benny didn't move to greet her; she didn't move at all. Sarah looked around the main room of the ICU where there was always at least one nurse at all times, and there was usually several. Across the room, Jimmy was standing where she was sure no one was standing before. He looked so happy. She started to go to him and ask him why Benny was here, but when she looked down Benny was gone, and then so was Jimmy.

"Sarah." She looked around for the voice. There was no one around.

"Sarah." Sarah hit her head on the arm of the chair as she woke up. She quickly realized where she was when the pain in her back and neck shot through her. She had been dreaming. It was nice. She would like Benny to be here. Somehow, curling up against her soft fur was always comforting and safe.

"Sarah." A hoarse voice spoke again. She wasn't asleep this time. She nearly fell as she jumped up out of the chairs with the blanket twisted around her.

"Jess, baby." She looked down into Jessica's beautiful black eyes, open for the first time in days.

"Where...am...I?" She spoke soft and scratchy so Sarah could barely hear her.

"Sweetheart, you're in the hospital." Sarah reached for her good hand. "I have to tell the nurse. She'll call Dr. Lue. Oh my God! It's so good to hear your voice."

"You...are...mad...at...me." She struggled to get the words out.

"Oh, Jess. I'm so sorry. I was mean. I'm not mad. Please don't try to talk. I have to get the doctor."

Jessica put pressure on Sarah's hand. "Don't...leave."

"I won't leave. I'm right here."

"I'm the one who...who...is sorry." Jessica paused and tried to swallow. "I did to you what my mother did to me."

"No, sweetheart. You were only trying to help. Please don't try to talk. I'm just so glad you're awake." Sarah reached across Jessica for the emergency call button and pushed it.

Sheri came running to the door. She stopped a second, taking in the scene.

"Jessica! Hello. Welcome back," Sheri said softly as she bent over Jessica. "I'm Sheri. I'm the ICU nurse. How are you feeling?" As the second night shift nurse entered, Sheri said, "Dawn, page Dr. Lue." Sheri looked over at Sarah. "When did she wake up?"

"Just now I think." They looked down at Jessica who was fighting to stay awake.

"Jessica," Sheri said too loudly and then more softly. "Stay with us, honey. The doctor is going to need to do some tests. Do you understand me?"

Jessica again put slight pressure on Sarah's hand and nodded a little and then winced. She tried to speak. "Wat... wa...water."

"Can she have some water?" Sarah asked

"I'll get her some ice chips." Sheri whispered in Sarah's ear. "Tell her what happened and why she is here. She's struggling to put things in place. Be vague and don't provide the scary details."

Sarah nodded, and Sheri left to get the ice chips.

"Jess, baby, can you hear me?" Jessica had closed her eyes again.

She opened them and looked at Sarah. Sarah felt her weak fingers tighten around her hand again.

Sarah explained what had happened to Jessica nearly five days ago. She told her about the coma and stay in the hospital. She ended with, "I love you, Jess. I was so scared I'd lost you."

Sheri had given her a couple of small pieces of ice while Sarah talked to her. "My dad?"

"I'm so sorry." She looked down at her. "Jimmy and I have been here with you." Jimmy needed to know. "Sheri, does Jimmy know she's awake?"

"Yes. He's pacing the floor like a wild animal waiting for news."

"Bring him in. He needs to be here, too."

"I don't think it is a good idea to have too much going on in here while she has so much to process." Sheri looked at her cautiously, and all of a sudden, Sarah was scared again. "He's okay. I asked him if he wanted to come to the door, but he was happier in the lounge. He's a little uncomfortable with this, you know."

Sarah nodded. Jessica was fighting sleep, and Sarah was so scared she wouldn't wake up. "Should we keep her awake?"

"Yes, until Dr. Lue gets here. Just talk to her. I'll be right out here. Dr. Lue doesn't live far. She'll be here soon."

Jessica looked up at Sarah with probing eyes. "Thank you."

"You don't have to thank me." Tears ran down Sarah's cheek. "I'm so glad to see your beautiful eyes. I've been so worried." She paused. She couldn't think of a thing to say.

"Jess, I'm so sorry I kicked you out. I was scared. I was scared of getting close to someone again and losing them. You were just trying to help, and I pushed you away. And then I nearly lost you. I was even more scared. It made me realize how much I love you. Can you forgive me?"

"Forgive me?" Jessica croaked out.

"There's nothing to forgive." Sarah squeezed her hand and bent to kiss her cheek.

Jessica smiled a tiny smile.

Dr. Lue entered the room and they both looked up. "Hi, Jessica. I'm Dr. Barbara Lue. It's so good to finally meet you." She leaned over to look in Jessica's eyes, holding her chart in one arm. "Sarah, I'm going to run through a few tests." She turned back to Jessica. "Can you talk to me?"

"Yes," she said still soft and hoarse, but much clearer than her earlier words.

"Maybe you could step out for just a few minutes."

"No!" Jessica screeched and tried to move her other arm to hold onto Sarah with both hands, but then cried out as the pain shot through her arm.

Sarah touched her face, and Dr. Lue immediately responded. "Okay. She'll be right here. I do need your hand though."

Sarah moved to the bottom of the bed. Jessica's eyes followed her, pleading. "I'm right here, baby. Feel my hands on your legs."

Jessica nodded.

Dr. Lue went through a protocol asking Jessica questions and documenting everything. After completing the tests, she turned to Sarah. "She's completely conscious and fully aware. Frankly, I'm quite amazed at how aware she is. This is a good sign, but there could still be..."

"I know you're talking about me." Jessica spoke slowly and softly, but in her normal commanding way, she made herself heard. "Please talk to *me*."

They moved back to the head of the bed. Sarah took Jessica's hand again and felt her squeeze—a little tighter than before. Dr. Lue moved to the other side of the bed. "Jessica, I'm sorry. It's just a bit unusual for someone who's been through what you've been through to be so...awake."

"When can I...get out of here?" Again, she spoke slowly and methodically as if each word required effort.

Dr. Lue laughed at her. "We need to monitor you for a few days. There's a risk that you could go back into a coma. Your head injury is still serious. The swelling is down significantly, but we need to keep you here a while longer."

"Jess, I'll be right here. It's just so good to have you back. Let's not push it." Sarah smiled at her and caressed her arm.

"I feel really tired, but I don't want to sleep." She paused, getting her breath. "I've slept too long. I want to get out of here." Each time she spoke, her voice was a little stronger.

Dr. Lue looked up at Sarah. "How about a plan?" Sarah smiled knowing this was exactly what Jessica needed. She had to have something to focus on—a goal. Dr. Lue continued looking back at Jessica. "It's very early in the morning. Let's say you sleep for two or three hours, and then we wake you up and see if you can drink a little. Later today, we'll try getting something solid in you. Then if all goes well today, we'll try to get you up in a wheelchair and perhaps a few steps tomorrow. We'll get some of this stuff off of you."

"I want to walk today. There's nothing wrong with my legs, right?" She looked at Sarah.

Sarah desperately looked at the doctor for help.

"Jessica, I understand, but you have to trust me. You're still in a fragile state. You just came out of a coma caused by a traumatic brain injury."

Sarah took over. "Jess, I couldn't take it if you slipped back into a coma. We'll be out of here soon. I'll take you home, and Benny and I will take care of you until you're ready to go back to Chicago."

Jessica finally nodded accepting the situation. "Sarah, you said you love me?" There was a question in Jessica's voice, and Sarah was afraid. For the last five days she had been telling herself it didn't matter if Jessica loved her—all she wanted was for her to be okay. If Jessica didn't feel the same way, she would just celebrate her being alive and do her best to move on. Now she knew it did matter. Sarah needed Jessica, and she realized she might be left with nothing all over again. She sighed, trying to be thankful that she was okay even if she wasn't going to be with her. And how could she be with her? Their lives were hundreds of miles away from one another.

Dr. Lue spoke up before either of them could say a word. "Jessica, you should allow yourself to sleep a little. We'll wake you in two hours. I'm afraid you're going to find it a bit frustrating and difficult to get rest, but we will wake you regularly to check your reflexes until we are confident you are stable."

"I am very tired." She looked over at Sarah. "Were you just saying that because you were scared I would die or do you really love me?"

Sarah knew the answer she was about to give was risky, and she was about to expose herself in a way she hadn't done in a long time. "I love you, Jess, and somehow—I don't know how, but I want you in my life."

Jessica smiled, and in a groggy voice said, "I love you too, Sarah Jarrett."

❖

For the next twenty-four hours, Jessica slept, only waking when the nurse came in to check her vitals. Jimmy tried to convince Sarah to go home, but there was no changing her mind. She snuggled in her nest of blankets in her two chairs for another night, but the stress and worry had diminished greatly.

"Sarah, are you awake?" Jessica woke early.

"I am now." She climbed out of the chairs awkwardly and stood next to Jessica's bed. "Are you okay? Do you need something?"

"You. Climb in."

"Jess, they'll kick me out if I climb in an ICU bed."

"Just for a minute," she said.

Sarah carefully climbed in the bed with Jessica, avoiding IVs and injuries. "You okay? I'm not hurting you, am I?"

"I'm not a doll. I'm fine. Can I see her? I want to see a picture of Cheryl. I know that I'll probably be jealous of her, but I also know I'll probably come to love her, too, if only through your eyes."

"I'd like that."

"You feel nice lying next to me," Jessica said.

"Hmm, I've missed you so much." She lightly kissed Jessica's cheek. And they lay quietly together until Jessica heard Sarah's steady breathing.

Jessica put her finger up to her lips as the nurse walked in.

Judy said quietly. "Ms. Whitney, this is against hospital policy in the ICU. If the head nurse comes in, she'll have my ass. I'll give her another hour to sleep and then I'm going to make her get up, because we're taking you out of the ICU."

Jessica smiled and mouthed thank you.

❖

Jessica was moved to a regular hospital room and asked for her computer and her iPad. Sarah explained that they had been stolen. Her first reaction was anger. Jessica had been struggling between anger and relief every time she was able to pull a few more details from someone to fill in the gaps where her memory was still struggling. She realized most anything she had on her computer was backed up on the firm's main server and was again grateful that it was only a computer. She called Mattie and asked her to provide the specs from her last computer to the local computer store.

Within a few hours, Jimmy returned having dutifully picked up all the new computer equipment and everything she asked for from the hotel. She worked on her new computer until the nurse took it away from her. Then they had to endure her begging to get it back, and they finally gave in. She was walking a little every couple of hours, and again, the nurses had to fight to keep her in bed and to get her to push the call button for assistance to use the restroom. Sarah was sleeping in the bed with her and working in the shop for about four or five hours a day until she couldn't stand not knowing how she was doing.

"You know you could keep working and just call and ask me how I'm doing," Jessica said as Sarah returned before it was even dark outside. "You're already behind, and you'll blame me."

"I'm catching up," she lied. "What would you like for dinner? Jimmy is waiting for instructions."

"Let's walk out and talk to him. Then we can all eat together since he won't come in here." She started to get up.

"Dammit, Jess. This is why I can't stay in the shop. I have to worry all day that you're doing something stupid. Let me get the walker, and I'll help you."

"Just give me your arm. I hate that thing." Jessica was already standing before Sarah could get to her. "Besides, I'm fine." She wobbled slightly. Sarah reached her in time to grab her waist and steady her.

"Yeah, you're fine all right." Sarah held her, and they made their way to the lobby.

"Brenda says you've been a pain in the ass today. She had to take your computer twice so you would take a nap," Sarah said. "Jess, you have to do what they say so you can get out of here sooner. Do you hear me?"

"Yes. I hear you. I just feel so much better, and I have so much to do. I feel useless taking a nap like a kindergartener curling up on a little rug in the middle of the day."

They reached the lobby where Jimmy sat with a book. He was so absorbed, he didn't see them. He jumped up when he heard Jessica's voice. "Ma'am, are you ready for dinner? I'll get whatever you want."

"Jess thought we could all eat together tonight," Sarah said.

"Oh no, ma'am. I'll eat out here."

"We'll eat out here with you." Jessica moved over and kissed his cheek before sitting in the chair next to him.

"Is that good for you to sit out here?" Jimmy asked

"Would you guys quit treating me like a China doll?"

"Ma'am, no disrespect, but we almost lost you. I think we get a few more days of worrying about you and taking care of you."

Jessica sent a thankful look to Jimmy and stopped complaining.

"Ms. Whitney! You're killing me." Brenda, the head nurse, walked over to them. "Ms. Sarah, can't you keep her under control?"

"Are you kidding me?" Sarah laughed.

"Well, I have good news for you. Dr. Lue was here earlier when you were sleeping, and she said if everything still looks good in the morning, she'll let you go home tomorrow evening if there's someone to care for you while you recover."

"You'll come to my house," Sarah said.

"Sarah, I couldn't impose on you. You have work to do, and you don't have time to take care of me. I can hire someone to stay in the hotel with me until I can handle things on my own."

"First of all, we all know that's bullshit. Sorry, but you know you won't do what you're supposed to do and take care of yourself if you hire someone. I can put Benny on watch duty, and she won't let you get up without me to help you. Besides, I can probably get more work done just coming in to check on you every hour or so. Jess, it would be best for both of us."

"How would it impact our relationship? You having to take care of your new girlfriend full-time. I don't know. I don't think it's a good idea."

"Ms. Whitney, you know she's right. I could also help out. If Ms. Sarah doesn't mind, I could stay with you during the day while she works and fix you both meals and run errands."

"Perfect, Jimmy. It's done. If Dr. Lue says it's okay, you're coming to my house tomorrow." Sarah jumped out of the chair and went to Jessica and hugged her lightly.

"I don't get a say?"

Jimmy and Sarah both said no at the same time and laughed.

"Okay. If you're sure." She looked at Sarah.

Sarah leaned over and kissed her. "I'm sure."

"Jimmy, have the hotel pack up my stuff and take it to Ms. Sarah's as she has directed."

"Yes, ma'am. Shall I bring back some dinner when I return?"

They both nodded and watched Jimmy run off.

❖

"Jimmy, go ahead and pull up on the lawn so we're closer to the door."

"No, don't do that. I can walk. You two!"

Jimmy looked at Sarah.

"Don't look at her. You work for me." She was frustrated and said it more harshly than she meant. "I'm sorry. I just mean...I mean...please...thank you both so much for taking care of me, but please don't overdo it."

"Okay, Jess," Sarah said.

Jimmy parked and Sarah helped her out of the car, into the house, and to the bedroom. Patricia had sent her crew over to redecorate the room, and it was much brighter with light colored curtains. The dark, heavy ones were pulled aside, but they could still be closed to keep out the light for day sleeping if necessary. The new comforter was a dark burgundy, and there were fresh flowers and candles everywhere. There was a picture of Sarah and Jessica from Thanksgiving sitting on the nightstand.

"Patricia was here." Jessica smiled at Sarah. "It's beautiful."

"Maybe I did it?" Sarah said.

"Maybe, but my money's on Patricia."

"Your money is safe. Do you like it? She thought it would be nicer if it was a little brighter since you were going to have to spend so much time in here."

"I love it. She's brilliant. Thank you both." She reached for Sarah, but wobbled as she stepped forward.

Sarah caught her. "I think you've had enough for one day. You were working so hard to get out of that hospital, you haven't rested all day. Lie down. Jimmy and I will get the rest of the stuff, and I'll bring you something to eat a little later. You'll stay put?"

"Yes. I will." For once, she wasn't arguing. Sarah could tell the exhaustion was weighing her down. She was getting stronger each day, but she was also getting better at knowing and abiding by her limits. Sarah assisted her into the bed.

"I'll hear you if you need anything. Just holler." She looked around for Benny who was standing at the end of the bed watching. "Benny, you stay. Bark if she gets up."

"She won't do that. She doesn't know what you're saying."

"Don't test her." Sarah smiled. "Your stuff from the hotel—oh my God. Did you bring everything you own? No, don't answer that. It's in the right side of the closet." It was Cheryl's side. She was glad Jimmy put the stuff away.

"Are you okay with me here, Sarah? This is a lot."

Sarah sat on the side of the bed and held Jessica's hand. "My beautiful girl, I'm okay. I'm glad you're here. I don't know how we are going to figure us out with all the things we have in front of us, but I want to be with you. And right now, I want you to be well again, and I'm just glad I'm the one here to help you. Now rest."

"Me too."

Sarah walked out and Benny followed. "No, Benny. You have *work* to do." She patted her. "Go lie down, stay, and watch her." Benny turned and curled up on the rug on Jessica's side of the bed.

Jimmy and Sarah had finished everything and were having a cup of coffee in the kitchen. "You should just stay in the spare room. It has a good mattress and the bathroom is just across the hall. You wouldn't have to drive back and forth."

"No, ma'am. I wouldn't be comfortable staying here with you and Ms. Whitney. Just tell me what time to come in the morning."

"If you're sure."

He nodded.

"Eight is probably good. I'll get her breakfast and settled with her computer. You know we won't be able to keep her from working. I just don't want her getting up on her own. If she falls, well, you know. Once you get here, I'll head out to the shop. Are you sure you don't mind fixing lunch and dinner for us?"

"I'm anxious to be of some real help. I'm a pretty good cook. Is there anything you don't eat? I know most of Ms. Whitney's likes and dislikes."

"Jimmy, as someone who hates to cook, I learned long ago to eat whatever is put in front of me." She smiled.

"I'll do the shopping—"

He was interrupted by Benny's loud bark.

Sarah ran to the bedroom with Jimmy behind her just in time to catch Jessica starting to stand up. "What are you doing?"

"You have got to be kidding me? How did you teach her that? I can't believe it. I just need to go to the bathroom. I have some dignity left, don't I? Can't I go to the bathroom by myself?" Frustration was all over her face and tears streaked her face.

"Jimmy, I got this." He left the room. "I'll help you to the door, and I'll leave you in the bathroom. There are plenty of things to hold on to in there." Sarah helped her to the master bathroom and closed the door.

Seconds later, Jessica opened the door looking her beautiful fresh self. Even the bandage around her head didn't detract from her beauty. The bruising was fading and the scrapes were healing quickly. She was going to have a subtle scar above her eye, but she was starting to look like her normal gorgeous self. Her eyes were tired, though. It would still be a while before the impact of what happened to her was fully processed.

"Jess, I know this is hard. I just can't take a chance on you falling. You have to let us help you."

"I know. I won't do it again. You're right." She walked into Sarah's arms. "It's just…I'm not used to being taken care of."

"I know, honey. I know." Sarah held her and they went slowly back to the bed. "If you stay in the bed for the next two days and get help each time you need it, then I'll set you up in my office so you can see out a little better and can probably get more work done. I know I won't be able to keep you from working no matter what I do. I don't think Benny will understand what computer work is so she won't be able to stop you."

"She is an amazing dog."

Sarah reached down and patted Benny. "You sure are, aren't you, Bernadette?"

"Bernadette? Really?"

"Yep. Are you hungry?"

"No, but I am tired." She paused. "Please don't rub it in, but you're right. It's been a long day."

"I won't rub it in." She stroked her face lightly with the back of her hand. "I'll get you a glass of water." She kissed her. "Good night, babe."

"Good night. Thank you, Sarah." She settled down in the bed snuggled around the comforter. She was asleep before Sarah was back with the water.

"Come, Benny. You're off shift now." Benny followed her in the living room and curled up on her bed at the end of the couch. It had been a hard dog day, too.

"If she's okay, I'll leave you. You'll probably enjoy sleeping in your own bed tonight. I'll see you at eight." Jimmy opened the front door. Benny stood next to him and pushed her head in his leg. He bent to pet her. "She is an amazing dog."

"Yeah, she likes you," Sarah said as Jimmy pulled the door closed. "I'll see you in the morning."

It was still early so Sarah went to her office and sat at her computer. She wanted to respond to a few e-mails and work on a CAD drawing for an upcoming project. Her customers all understood when she explained the situation, and she had plenty of work. Now she just needed to get it done. She asked Christine to pick up the check from David and deposit it for her. She paid Joe in full and some other credit that had stacked up. She was in much better shape. As much as she didn't want to take Jessica's money, she needed to get some things paid off since she had spent so many days in the hospital. She would pay her back every penny—maybe one penny at a time. After working through all her e-mail, Sarah felt quite satisfied, but she had lost track of time. It was nearly midnight. She had to get some sleep. Her new routine starting tomorrow might take some getting used to. Sarah walked out of her office to pull Benny off her normal night watch duty for a potty break.

Benny wasn't lying in front of the door. Sarah looked in her bed, and she wasn't there either. Sarah panicked for a minute before she went to the bedroom and saw Benny curled up on the rug next to Jessica's side of the bed.

Sarah lay down on the floor with her. "Can we move on now, Benny?" A tear slid down her face. Benny licked it off her cheek.

"Sarah, is that you? Where are you?" Jessica woke.

Sarah patted Benny's head and got up off the floor and climbed into the bed next to her. "I'm right here, baby…with you."

About the Author

Jan Gayle was raised in a small farming community in central Illinois. Upon graduating from college with a B.S. in social studies education, Jan joined the U.S. Air Force. She later accepted a commission and served for twenty years as an Air Force officer. As a new lieutenant, she deployed to Desert Storm. She returned to the Middle East for another deployment to Operation Iraqi Freedom fourteen years later. While on active duty, Jan visited over forty countries and was assigned to locations all over the United States. She continues to work for the Air Force as a civil servant, but her true passion is her small woodworking business where she builds custom wood furniture. Jan lives with her wife Jules and their two boys. She started writing on a dare and was immediately hooked. *Live and Love Again* is Jan's debut novel.

Jan can be contacted at: jggourley@gmail.com
Website: www.froggybuilder.com/
Twitter: www.twitter.com/@jggourley

Books Available from Bold Strokes Books

Dyre: By Moon's Light by Rachel E. Bailey. A young werewolf, Des, guards the aging leader of all the Packs: the Dyre. Stable employment—nice work, if you can get it...at least until silver bullets start to fly. (978-1-62639-6-623)

Fragile Wings by Rebecca S. Buck. In Roaring Twenties London, can Evelyn Hopkins find love with Jos Singleton or will the scars of the Great War crush her dreams? (978-1-62639-5-466)

Live and Love Again by Jan Gayle. Jessica Whitney could be Sarah Jarret's second chance at love, but their differences and Sarah's grief continue to come between their budding relationship. (978-1-62639-5-176)

Starstruck by Lesley Davis. Actress Cassidy Hayes and writer Aiden Darrow find out the hard way not all life-threatening drama is confined to the TV screen or the pages of a manuscript. (978-1-62639-5-237)

Stealing Sunshine by Tina Michele. Under the Central Florida sun, two women struggle between fear and love as a dangerous plot of deception and revenge threatens to steal priceless art and lives. (978-1-62639-4-452)

The Fifth Gospel by Michelle Grubb. Hiding a Vatican secret is dangerous—sharing the secret suicidal—can Felicity survive a perilous book tour, and will her PR specialist, Anna, be there when it's all over? (978-1-62639-4-476)

Cold to the Touch by Cari Hunter. A drug addict's murder is the start of a dangerous investigation for Detective Sanne Jensen and Dr. Meg Fielding, as they try to stop a killer with no conscience. (978-1-62639-526-8)

Forsaken by Laydin Michaels. The hunt for a killer teaches one woman that she must overcome her fear in order to love, and another that success is meaningless without happiness. (978-1-62639-481-0)

Infiltration by Jackie D. When a CIA breach is imminent, a Marine instructor must stop the attack while protecting her heart from being disarmed by a recruit. (978-1-62639-521-3)

Midnight at the Orpheus by Alyssa Linn Palmer. Two women desperate to make their way in the world, a man hell-bent on revenge, and a cop risking his career: all in a day's work in Capone's Chicago. (978-1-62639-607-4)

Spirit of the Dance by Mardi Alexander. Major Sorla Reardon's return to her family farm to heal threatens Riley Johnson's safe life when small-town secrets are revealed, and love may not conquer all. (978-1-62639-583-1)

Sweet Hearts by Melissa Brayden, Rachel Spangler, and Karis Walsh. Do you ever wonder *Whatever happened to...*? Find out when you reconnect with your favorite characters from Melissa Brayden's *Heart Block*, Rachel Spangler's *LoveLife*, and Karis Walsh's *Worth the Risk*. (978-1-62639-475-9)

Totally Worth It by Maggie Cummings. Who knew there's an all-lesbian condo community in the NYC suburbs? Join twentysomething BFFs Meg and Lexi at Bay West as they navigate friendships, love, and everything in between. (978-1-62639-512-1)

Illicit Artifacts by Stevie Mikayne. Her foster mother's death cracked open a secret world Jil never wanted to see...and now she has to pick up the stolen pieces. (978-1-62639-472-8)

Pathfinder by Gun Brooke. Heading for their new homeworld, Exodus's chief engineer Adina Vantressa and nurse Briar Lindemay carry game-changing secrets that may well cause them to lose everything when disaster strikes. (978-1-62639-444-5)

Prescription for Love by Radclyffe. Dr. Flannery Rivers finds herself attracted to the new ER chief, city girl Abigail Remy, and the incendiary mix of city and country, fire and ice, tradition and change is combustible. (978-1-62639-570-1)

Ready or Not by Melissa Brayden. Uptight Mallory Spencer finds relinquishing control to bartender Hope Sanders too tall an order in fast-paced New York City. (978-1-62639-443-8)

Summer Passion by MJ Williamz. Women loving women is forbidden in 1946 Hollywood, yet Jean and Maggie strive to keep their love alive and away from prying eyes. (978-1-62639-540-4)

The Princess and the Prix by Nell Stark. "Ugly duckling" Princess Alix of Monaco was resigned to loneliness until she met racecar driver Thalia d'Angelis. (978-1-62639-474-2)

Winter's Harbor by Aurora Rey. Lia Brooks isn't looking for love in Provincetown, but when she discovers chocolate croissants and pastry chef Alex McKinnon, her winter retreat quickly starts heating up. (978-1-62639-498-8)

The Time Before Now by Missouri Vaun. Vivian flees a disastrous affair, embarking on an epic, transformative journey to escape her past, until destiny introduces her to Ida, who helps her rediscover trust, love, and hope. (978-1-62639-446-9)

Twisted Whispers by Sheri Lewis Wohl. Betrayal, lies, and secrets—whispers of a friend lost to darkness. Can a reluctant psychic set things right or will an evil soul destroy those she loves? (978-1-62639-439-1)

The Courage to Try by C.A. Popovich. Finding love is worth getting past the fear of trying. (978-1-62639-528-2)

Break Point by Yolanda Wallace. In a world readying for war, can love find a way? (978-1-62639-568-8)

Countdown by Julie Cannon. Can two strong-willed, powerful women overcome their differences to save the lives of seven others and begin a life they never imagined together? (978-1-62639-471-1)

Keep Hold by Michelle Grubb. Claire knew some things should be left alone and some rules should never be broken, but the most forbidden, well, they are the most tempting. (978-1-62639-502-2)

Deadly Medicine by Jaime Maddox. Dr. Ward Thrasher's life is in turmoil. Her partner Jess left her, and her job puts her in the path of a murderous physician who has Jess in his sights. (978-1-62639-424-7)

New Beginnings by KC Richardson. Can the connection and attraction between Jordan Roberts and Kirsten Murphy be enough for Jordan to trust Kirsten with her heart? (978-1-62639-450-6)

Officer Down by Erin Dutton. Can two women who've made careers out of being there for others in crisis find the strength to need each other? (978-1-62639-423-0)

Reasonable Doubt by Carsen Taite. Just when Sarah and Ellery think they've left dangerous careers behind, a new case sets them—and their hearts—on a collision course. (978-1-62639-442-1)

Tarnished Gold by Ann Aptaker. Cantor Gold must outsmart the Law, outrun New York's dockside gangsters, outplay a shady art dealer, his lover, and a beautiful curator, and stay out of a killer's gun sights. (978-1-62639-426-1)

White Horse in Winter by Franci McMahon. Love between two women collides with the inner poison of a closeted horse trainer in the green hills of Vermont. (978-1-62639-429-2)

Autumn Spring by Shelley Thrasher. Can Bree and Linda, two women in the autumn of their lives, put their hearts first and find the love they've never dared seize? (978-1-62639-365-3)

The Renegade by Amy Dunne. Post-apocalyptic survivors Alex and Evelyn secretly find love while held captive by a deranged cult, but when their relationship is discovered, they must fight for their freedom—or die trying. (978-1-62639-427-8)

Thrall by Barbara Ann Wright. Four women in a warrior society must work together to lift an insidious curse while caught between their own desires, the will of their peoples, and an ancient evil. (978-1-62639-437-7)

The Chameleon's Tale by Andrea Bramhall. Two old friends must work through a web of lies and deceit to find themselves again, but in the search they discover far more than they ever went looking for. (978-1-62639-363-9)

Side Effects by VK Powell. Detective Jordan Bishop and Dr. Neela Sahjani must decide if it's easier to trust someone with your heart or your life as they face threatening protestors, corrupt politicians, and their increasing attraction. (978-1-62639-364-6)

Warm November by Kathleen Knowles. What do you do if the one woman you want is the only one you can't have? (978-1-62639-366-0)

In Every Cloud by Tina Michele. When Bree finally leaves her shattered life behind, is she strong enough to salvage the remaining pieces of her heart and find the place where it truly fits? (978-1-62639-413-1)